"WAS THERE EVER SOMETHING YOU WANTED SO BADLY YOU THOUGHT YOU'D DIE IF YOU DIDN'T GET IT?"

Mother thought a minute, and then she said, "There was a boy I felt that way about."

"And what did you do?"

"I suffered."

"Mother, you've got to let me save Zoro. You've got to."

Her mother gave her a sympathetic look. "Betsy, you've got to stop breaking your heart over all the poor dogs in the world—and cats and gerbils and guinea pigs."

"Zoro's not just any dog. At least come with me and see him. Would you do that at least?"

"No, I'm tired. I've had a long day already and I just am not able to put myself through any more."

"You can do anything if it's for Pops or Hal, but nothing I want is important. I don't count for anything in this family," Besty said, too upset to care how tired her mother was. The whole family treated her like a baby but she would show them. Zoro was counting on her and Betsy would save him with or without her parents' help . . .

Books from SIGNET VISTA

- [ ] **A BOAT TO NOWHERE by Maureen Crane Wartski**
  (W9678—$1.50)*
- [ ] **RUN, DON'T WALK by Harriet May Savitz.** (#AE1488—$1.75)
- [ ] **A FIVE-COLOR BUICK AND A BLUE-EYED CAT by Phyllis Anderson Wood.** (#Y9109—$1.25)
- [ ] **I THINK THIS IS WHERE I CAME IN by Phyllis Anderson Wood.** (#AW1482—$1.50)
- [ ] **I'VE MISSED A SUNSET OR THREE by Phyllis Anderson Wood.** (#Y7944—$1.25)
- [ ] **SONG OF THE SHAGGY CANARY by Phyllis Anderson Wood.** (#W9793—$1.50)
- [ ] **ADVENTURES IN DARKNESS by Derek Gill.** (#W7698—$1.50)
- [ ] **THE BETRAYAL OF BONNIE by Barbara Van Tuyl.** (#W8879—$1.50)
- [ ] **BONNIE AND THE HAUNTED FARM by Barbara Van Tuyl.** (#AE1184—$1.75)
- [ ] **A HORSE CALLED BONNIE by Pat Johnson and Barbara Van Tuyl.** (#Y7728—$1.25)
- [ ] **ELLEN GRAE AND LADY ELLEN by Vera and Bill Cleaver.** (#J7832—$1.95)
- [ ] **I WOULD RATHER BE A TURNIP by Vera and Bill Cleaver.** (#W9539—$1.50)
- [ ] **ME TOO by Vera and Bill Cleaver.** (#Y6519—$1.25)
- [ ] **GROVER by Vera and Bill Cleaver.** (#AE1313—$1.95)
- [ ] **THE WHYS AND WHEREFORES OF LITTABELLE LEE by Vera and Bill Cleaver.** (#Y7225—$1.25)
- [ ] **WHERE THE LILIES BLOOM by Vera and Bill Cleaver.** (#W8065—$1.50)

*Price slightly higher in Canada.

SHELTER ON BLUE BARNS ROAD

BY C. S. ADLER

A SIGNET VISTA BOOK

NEW AMERICAN LIBRARY

TIMES MIRROR

PUBLISHER'S NOTE

This novel is a work of fiction. Names, characters, places, and incidents are either the product of the author's imagination or are used fictitiously, and any resemblance to actual persons, living or dead, events, or locales is entirely coincidental.

RL 3.5/IL 5+

 SIGNET VISTA TRADEMARK REG. U.S. PAT. OFF. AND FOREIGN COUNTRIES REGISTERED TRADEMARK—MARCA REGISTRADA HECHO EN CHICAGO, IL., U.S.A.

SIGNET, SIGNET CLASSICS, MENTOR, PLUME, MERIDIAN AND NAL BOOKS are published by The New American Library, Inc., 1633 Broadway, New York, New York 10019

First Signet Vista Printing, March, 1982

1 2 3 4 5 6 7 8 9

PRINTED IN THE UNITED STATES OF AMERICA

F
ADL

In memory of Betsy,
who loved animals

Thanks are due to James Provost,
Manager of the Schenectady Animal Shelter,
Alplaus Road, Schenectady, New York 12301,
and to Nancy Lyon
for their cooperation and information.

Chapter One

A barking dog woke Betsy. She rolled out of bed and looked out the window. Nothing out there but a bare yard of mangy grass with a few trees screening an old barn that had once been painted blue. The barn looked interesting, but she doubted it was on their property. Beyond the barn, she glimpsed a one-story, factorylike structure. Another dog yipped out of tune with the first. At least dogs were out there to make friends with even if there weren't any humans. Here in this upstate New York countryside, houses kept their distance from one another. There was no stoop to sit on for easy meeting and greeting of passersby. No stickball games to join in the street the way there had been in Brooklyn. No street—just empty roads.

She eased up the screen and estimated the distance to the ground. A short drop. Good. She'd have her own private exit, then. The sun was two hands above the horizon on this chilly, April-blue morning. Probably her mother had already left for work and Pops and Hal were still sleeping. Betsy pulled yesterday's jeans and shirt onto her thin body and climbed out the window. She was eager to explore. Maybe a best friend was waiting for her in some house beyond the trees, somebody who wasn't always getting mad and wouldn't always drop her for another kid the way Phoebe had had a habit of doing. "Why do you let that girl use you?" Betsy's mother had asked. "Haven't you learned yet that Phoebe only cares about Phoebe?" Mother was right. Phoebe was not the ideal best friend. But then, Mother was always right, and Phoebe had been a kind of friend at least, better than no friend at all.

Betsy rounded the corner of the sagging barn and stopped to sniff a pungent odor. It came from the soft earth under her feet. Old manure pile maybe? The barn door was latched with a long iron bar that she shoved at but couldn't quite budge. The sudden whining of a dog begging for something caught her attention, and she let the bar be and headed for the sound. It seemed to be coming from the squat, cinder-block building that looked like a factory. Now she could see a line-up of cages along the back of the building. Every cage held a dog. Immediately she cheered up.

Her mother had once accused her of loving dogs more than people. Betsy denied it. She couldn't help believing, though, that dogs were nicer than people.

Was this place an animal hospital, a kennel, or what? She drifted closer to the cages, drawn by the whining and the abrupt *yip-yip-yip* of another dog. Not a person in sight. If the place was a kennel, it didn't specialize in any particular breed. In fact, the dogs in the cages were mostly mongrels. An animal hospital, then, and these were pets boarded while their owners were on vacation? Except these dogs looked so uncared for—dull coats and droopy tails. They watched her coming to them with sorrowful eyes. The bones on one brown-spotted pointer showed pitifully. Two puppies with diaper-shaped ears huddled together at the back of their cage, shivering in the cool morning air. One small reddish dog with a foxy face barked threateningly at her and clawed the front of his cage to get at her. With all that noise, Betsy kept expecting someone to appear, but nobody came. Something about the place made her uneasy. It was as neglected as a dingy alley where anything could happen.

In the center of one cage stood a sleek black, pointy-eared Doberman with brown fur lining his undersides and half circles of brown above his intelligent eyes. Ears at attention, he watched her intently. His dignity impressed her—the way he stood so quietly. She wondered that he was caged in this shabby place. Whoever owned him had to be pretty careless to leave him here. She leaned against the steel wire of his cage and twined her fingers through, calling to him softly, "Here, boy. Here, handsome. Here, boy."

The Doberman stood slim and alert, like an athlete waiting for the starting gun. His honey-colored eyes never left her face. "Here, boy," she called. She knelt in front of the cage, pressing her face wistfully to the worm-thick wires. "Here, boy." Something about him stirred her. Her heart twisted in sympathy for him. He was a prince, a captured prince. "Here, boy," she coaxed. Finally he took two steps toward her and lowered his moist, inquisitive nose to sniff at her fingers, her face. Long minutes passed while he spoke to her with his eyes, confiding in her wordlessly, and the other dogs, seeing her concentration, fell quiet. It was just the Doberman and Betsy in silent communion.

"Hi, you," she whispered to him. "Were you waiting for me? Do you want to be my special friend?" She felt dizzy with a sudden upsurge of love.

The warmth of the sun was like a tap on her shoulder, reminding her she'd better get home before they missed her. No sense getting them mad at her. Today she and Hal were to help Pops unpack while Mother put in her first day on the new job. Reluctantly she told the Doberman, "Bye for now. I'll come back and see you later. O.K.?"

He watched her go as if her leaving were no surprise to him, as if he were too proud to ask for more. It grieved her when she looked back to see him standing there so silently, looking after her. "I'll be back," she promised, and retraced her steps past the barn.

Two cinder blocks lay in the tall grass at the back of her yard. She lugged them to her bedroom window so that she could stand on them and heave herself back over the windowsill. She could have gone around to the front door, of course, but she liked her secret entrance better. She made her bed the way she always did, just pulling the bedspread over the rumpled blanket and sheets, then headed down the hall of the three-bedroom ranch house.

Through the open door of her seventeen-year-old brother's room, she could see his body mummified in his comforter in the middle of the bare double bed. As usual, pillow, bedspread, clothes and other possessions littered the floor. Hal couldn't see keeping his room neat, no matter how much Mother nagged him. He kept himself neat, though, always looking well dressed even in jeans and a shirt with rolled-up sleeves.

Betsy crept over to his bed, leaped and landed astride his wrapped middle shouting, "Wake-up time!"

"Yow!" he yelled and jerked upright to flail at her through the comforter. "Betsy, you little witch. When are you going to grow up and start acting human?"

She rolled off his bed and said, "Aren't you going to get up and help Pops and me with the unpacking? I've been waiting for you for hours."

"I'll bet you have." His eyelids were puffed with sleep in his otherwise handsome face. "I'll bet you just rolled out of bed yourself."

"It's nice out, Hal. Come for a walk with me before we start working."

"Go walk yourself. I'm gonna look for a job."

"You're not going to help unpack?"

"Soon as I get some applications in, I'll come back and do my part. But if I'm gonna start high school tomorrow, I've gotta use today for job-hunting."

"You didn't have a job in Brooklyn."

"No. Dad had one, though."

"He couldn't help it that he lost his job, Hal."

"Couldn't he? That's a matter of opinion."

She couldn't argue with him. She was just his little sister, someone to be teased and tolerated, not a person to be listened to seriously. But she knew he'd been mad at Pops ever since Pops had been asked to leave his teaching job midway through the year because of parents' complaints. It wasn't Pops's fault. The kids had driven him out of his mind, so he'd shoved a couple around and used bad language. Hal said having to switch schools at the end of his junior year meant he had no chance for a sports scholarship to college now.

Never mind that Mother had told him not to worry, that they would see to it he didn't miss out on college. He'd answered her with sarcasm. "You will, Mom? On what? Just your salary? What are you going to pay the grocery bills with, then?"

"That's your father's and my concern, not yours," Mother had answered.

But Hal was a worrying type. He always planned everything carefully in advance and took any obstacle that got in his way as a personal insult.

"Will you take me to town with you if you're going?" Betsy asked him now.

"Can't, Betsy. I don't have time. Go 'way now so I can get dressed."

She found her father sitting at the kitchen table, apparently studying the steam rising from the cup of coffee in front of him. Boxes of their belongings were stacked like squat totem poles in awkward places. She crept up behind him and clapped her hands over his eyes. "Guess who?"

"Betsy, you know I hate that." He removed her hands from his eyes none too gently.

Bad mood, she thought. He'd been in a bad mood most of the time lately, not just since he'd lost his teaching job, either. He'd been wrapped in the cocoon of his own thoughts for months, down about something, nothing he'd talk to her about. Why did she have to be born the baby, four years younger than Hal? Betsy poured herself a glass of milk, drank, and broke off a piece of cheese on which to nibble. "Pops, how's about we go for a walk? It's so beautiful out this morning."

"Can't. We have to unpack."

"A walk first would pep us up."

"Your mother expects us to be working productively, not lollygagging around having a good time while she brings home the bacon."

"She won't know. We'll gets lots done when we come back."

"Get off my back, Betsy."

He hadn't raised his eyes once from the coffee cup. It was really bad this morning. She put her arms around him and rubbed her cheek against his grizzled one. "Don't feel bad, Popsy. Something good will turn up for you."

He didn't say anything, but he reached around her and squeezed her arm affectionately, still staring into the black well of coffee. No more steam now. She considered, eyeing the boxes. "I don't mind doing my share, but I hate to work alone," she said.

"Don't nag. Why do women always nag so much?"

"Well, are you going to help?"

"When I'm ready."

"Maybe I'll go for a walk, then, and come back later."

He didn't object. All he said was, "I hate this godforsaken place. Why did we move here?"

"Because Mother finally got a full-time job as a

guidance counselor here," she answered him, as if the question really were directed at her.

"Right, and it's O.K. if Mother brings home the bacon for a while while Father takes stock of himself and resets his course in life. That's acceptable practice nowadays, the norm, you might say."

"Sure, Popsy."

"Sure, sure. Betsy, I'm not in the mood for working yet. Why don't you go read a book or something for a while?"

"I guess I'll go out and look around," she said.

He ought to know she never read unless she had to for school. She was dumb, a solid C student. Her parents couldn't understand it. They were so smart, and Hal brought home A's and B's even with all the athletics he'd been involved in. Pops had once joked, "Maybe she's a changeling." She'd looked that up in the dictionary and been hurt. A changeling was a child secretly put in place of another by the fairies. "Witchy girl," Hal called her when he wanted to make her mad. She did look witchy to herself when she looked in the mirror. Sometimes she would look and look, trying to see some of the regular-featured handsomeness Hal and Pops had. But the two sides of her face didn't match, and her mouth was too big, and her eyes were only ordinary brown, not beautiful dark moons like her mother's.

She ran from the house, only stopping to catch her breath when she was in sight of the cages again. Then she considered going back to cheer up her father. When she was little, he used to say nobody could cheer him up the way she could. But ever since she'd gotten to be the same age as the kids he'd taught, he liked her less. "Little monsters," he called his students. "The monsters were out to get me today. I couldn't get control of that fifth-period class no matter what I did." He had been known as an easy teacher.

"Your father lets kids get away with anything," her friend Phoebe had reported to Betsy once.

"He does not!" Betsy had protested, as if defending his reputation could change anything. It hurt her to know that kids acted up in her father's class just to see how far they could push him. Making him lose his temper was a big joke to them.

"Your father can't teach," a boy had taunted Betsy in the cafeteria.

"My father's a great teacher," Betsy had answered. "You're just too dumb to appreciate him." When the boy had laughed, she'd hit him in the gut and got detention from the principal for it. She had told her mother about the detention, but not Pops, even though she would have liked him to know she had defended him. No, he didn't need her. No one needed her. She was an unnecessary person, not smart, not pretty. No wonder she didn't even have a true friend.

The Doberman stepped right up to the front of the cage when she crouched down to greet him again. He panted a little, with his mouth open and his pink tongue out. He seemed to be listening to everything she was telling him about where she had gone and why she'd been able to come back so soon to see him. He jumped back, though, when she poked a finger through the wires to touch him. "I'm not going to hurt you, handsome," she said, surprised that he was so timid. "What's wrong? You're not afraid of *me*, are you? I'm your friend."

"Hey, you! Kid! Get away from there. That dog bites."

She looked over her shoulder. A boy of about sixteen was waving her frantically away from the cage. He was bone thin as she was, but tall, black-haired and fair-skinned with uptilted Oriental eyes and a generous mouth. Chinese, she thought, but just the eyes. The rest of him was loose-limbed American.

"Don't worry. He wouldn't bite me," Betsy said.

"You're wrong. He's already bitten two people. That's why he's here."

"What? What is this place, anyway? An obedience school?"

"Didn't you read the sign out front? This is the animal shelter, the Blue Barns Road Animal Shelter."

"So that's why all these dogs are here," she said. "How long do they stay?"

"Depends. Not long if their owner comes to claim them. Longer until somebody comes in to adopt them if they're strays."

"Is this dog a stray?"

"Him? No. We'll probably have to get rid of him."

"What do you mean, get rid of him?"

The boy's eyes evaded hers, going to the cages and then to the bucket and shovel in his hands. "I've got to get to work," he said. "You better get out of here. No visitors allowed until one o'clock. Mr. Berrier is strict about the rules."

"Who's Mr. Berrier?"

"My boss, the guy who manages the shelter. Come back at one if you're interested in getting a dog—but not that one."

"Do most of the dogs get adopted?" she persisted, looking into the patient eyes of the black dog who was still concentrating on her as if she were the only person in the world.

"No. Only about half."

"Then what do you do with the rest?"

"Look—" he said impatiently.

"Tell me and I'll go."

"It's a fact of life," he said. "The way things are. There's just more dogs than people want— cats, too—so they wander around homeless until they starve to death or get hit by a car or they wind up here, and then if they don't get lucky, we end up having to put them down."

"Put them down?" She couldn't believe what she was thinking. "You don't mean you *kill* them?"

Her horror must have been obvious because he

said, "Sometimes we have to. Look, we only do what has to be done. People should have their animals fixed so that they can't produce all those puppies and kittens nobody wants."

"What kind of kid are you?" she cried. "Don't you like animals?"

"Sure I do. What else would I work here for? The pay's nothing, and believe me, the work's not much fun. Hey, you know, I already told you twice to get out of here?"

"This dog"—she pointed to the Doberman—"he won't be 'put down,' will he?"

"Not for a while. He's only been here a few days. His owner died, an old lady who had an appliance store a quarter of a mile down the road from here. She used that Doberman to guard the store nights. He even made the paper once. Two guys broke in, and by the time the police got there, they were chewed up so bad that the police took them to the hospital instead of jail."

"The dog was doing his job, then, wasn't he?"

"But he's a killer. That old lady got him from a man who starved and beat him to make him mean. Nobody's going to want a dog who hates people."

"He doesn't hate me and I'm going to adopt him," she decided out loud. "You will keep him for me until I can adopt him, won't you?"

"You've gotta talk to Mr. Berrier about that. I don't have anything to do with the adopting."

"Just the killing," she said bitterly.

"I do the feeding and the cleaning up, sometimes the nursing when they're sick, but sometimes—yeah, somebody has to do it."

"No, that's not true."

"Oh, go home, kid. You know you're a pest? Go on home." She understood his anger. She had made him feel guilty.

"I'll come back at one and talk to Mr. Berrier," she said. She looked down the line of cages. They knew. All those shivering, pleading, hopeless animals knew they were in a trap. She looked into the honey-colored eyes of the Doberman, her captured prince. Now she knew what he was asking her. "Save me!" She was the only one who understood him. His life was in her hands. Somehow she had to rescue him.

She turned around and raced back past the barn, across the yard, through the unlocked front door of her house. Her father was sitting in his chair in the living room, listening to one of his doleful classical records with his head buried in his hands.

"Popsy!" she said, but he didn't even look up.

She hurtled down the hall and threw herself onto her own bed. An animal shelter! What a laugh that was. "Animal shelter" for a place that killed dogs. She closed her eyes and tried to find a hiding place inside her head, but the horror crept in after her. She wondered if there were other shelters, if all over the country animals were being "put down" because no one wanted them. The idea sickened her. She got up and began pacing around her bedroom, biting on her knuckles. First she had to save the Doberman. Then she would see what she could do for those others.

Chapter Two

Later that morning she helped her father unpack some of the boxes of kitchen utensils, but he complained so bitterly about the junk they had brought and what it showed about the poor quality of their lives that she didn't tell him about the Doberman. Finally he took notice of her. "What're you looking so miserable about, Betsy?" he asked.

"I found something awful this morning," she began in a rush.

He put his hand out like a traffic cop to stop her. "I don't want to hear about anything awful. In case you haven't noticed, I'm not feeling too chipper myself. Tell you what. Let's take time off from our labors. You can go get some fresh air."

She didn't need to be told twice. It was after one, time to speak to Mr. Berrier. Though she had no idea what to say. She could continue the lie she'd started this morning, but how far would that get her?

This time she circled the concrete block building and passed the cages that lined the front of the shelter facing the highway. She didn't allow herself to look at the dogs that barked or yelped or jumped about, trying to get her attention. They tugged hard at her sympathies, but she focused herself on her mission, which according to Hal was the only way to get anything done. The blue letters on the white sign near the road said *Blue Barns Road Animal Shelter*. The very attractiveness of the sign was a lie that made Betsy angry.

She carried her indignation into the entryway. To her left was a high counter with no one behind it. To her right stood two tattered kitchen chairs and a table with pamphlets on heart worm, care of puppies and kittens and rules for adoption. Betsy walked around the counter to the open doorway of an office where a stocky, gray-haired man with a square, creased face sat at a battered desk talking on the phone. Betsy had no doubt he was Mr. Berrier. A rooster-sized Pomeranian lying on a telephone book on the desk yipped nastily at her. The man finished his conversation and said, "What can I do for you, honey?"

"I want to adopt the Doberman."

"You do, huh? The Doberman? You mean Zoro?"

"If that's his name."

"Well, Zoro's the only Doberman we got right now. Nice-looking dog, but you don't want him, honey."

"He's the only dog I want."

"Well, ordinarily I'd say fine. Ordinarily. But that's one vicious dog. I couldn't in all conscience let him go as a pet. Guard dog, maybe, if the right party came along, someone who could handle him. But he'd never make it as a pet. They did too good a job on him when he was a pup, worked him over till he was scared mean."

"He likes me."

"Well, that could be. Anything's possible. I've seen stranger things than a dog just picking out some special person to like, but even if he took to you—which I sort of doubt—you couldn't ever trust him with anybody else."

"I plan to retrain him."

"Uh huh. Well, you bring your folks in, and if they give permission— You gotta have an adult to sign the papers, see? That's the rule. And it'll cost you thirty-five dollars because he is a purebred Doberman, plus ten dollars deposit for the neutering which you get back when that's taken care of. . . . Maybe you should just look around now, though, and see if there's another dog you like. We got a real gentle beagle would make a fine pet for a little girl like you."

"I'm not little. I'm thirteen."

"Oh, right. Thirteen." He nodded.

"I've already picked Zoro," she said. "You won't—I mean, you'll keep him for me at least?"

He nodded. "Sure, we'll put a hold on Zoro for you. Though I don't think you're going to have much competition. Nobody wants a dog that bites. Course, you can never tell. Just this morning a lady come in. We had a poodle here, mixed breed, funny-looking fellow with a long setter's tail, barked so much it nearly drove us crazy. Well, we were going to put him down today, but that lady thought he was the cutest thing she'd ever seen. She was deaf. So she couldn't hear him. So it worked out good after all. Sometimes it happens like that." He reached out a meaty hand to pet the Pomeranian.

"He's cute," Betsy said. "Is he yours?"

"Belongs here," Mr. Berrier said. "The shelter's mascot. He's a little spitfire. Bites anybody who tries to pet him except the employees of the shelter. Don't know how he tells the new workers, but he does. He's had the run of the place for a couple of years now, ever since he sort of adopted us."

She looked enviously at the small arrogant face of the plumy-tailed Pomeranian. Why him and not Zoro? She was about to ask how Mr. Berrier tolerated a mascot that bit after what he had just said about Zoro when a long-haired young man with a drooping mustache appeared at the counter. He cleared his throat to get Mr. Berrier's attention.

"You take in dogs here?" the young man asked.

"Right," Mr. Berrier said, rising to take his position at his side of the counter.

"I got a golden retriever here. I can't keep her," the young man said casually. "My landlord changed."

"Uh huh," Mr. Berrier said, getting out a card and beginning to make notations. "How old is she?"

"Nine months."

"Any bad habits?"

"No, she's a nice dog, very friendly."

Betsy ducked around the counter to see a large dog the color of baked bread crust standing quietly beside the young man. When she bent and petted the dog, it licked her face.

"Shots?" Mr. Berrier asked.

"No. I didn't get her none."

"She been spayed?"

"No. She's a good dog, though. Someone will probably give her a home, huh?"

"Ummm."

The young man nodded, not seeming to need further reassurance. He signed the paper Mr. Berrier proferred, said, "Stay, Sheila," to the dog and ambled out without a backward glance. The dog stayed put, looking after her master.

Betsy couldn't believe what she had just seen. "He didn't even care!" she cried.

"You'd be surprised how many don't. They get a puppy, keep him for a while, then dump him when they get tired of him. Looks like this one's a nice dog, too." Mr. Berrier shrugged. "How about this one, honey? Wouldn't you like a nice golden retriever like this?"

She bit her lip, wanting to say yes, wanting both, every dog in the shelter if she could have them. But Zoro was the one who needed her. He had picked her out to trust, her alone among all the humans he knew, and she would never let him down. "I'll come back about Zoro," she said.

The phone rang. Mr. Berrier picked it up. "Animal shelter. . . . Where was the dog hit? . . . Yeah, we'll send a van. Be about half an hour."

She backed out unobtrusively and drifted down the long corridor smelling of ammonia and eerily lit with fluorescent lights overhead. The empty inside cages flanked the wet concrete walk where an endless hose lay ready. She stopped at a room to the right. There cats were stacked in box cages three high. The silent room full of watchful eyes made her heart sink. What could she do to help them? How could people be so rotten they dumped their pets when they got tired of them, leaving them to be "put down" as if they were garbage? Zoro! She knew her parents would never let her adopt him. All of a sudden she couldn't stand it. She whirled and ran home. This time they had to listen to her. She'd make them adopt Zoro.

Chapter Three

She knew her father would be easier to convince than her mother. He caved in under nagging. Mother held firm, reasonable and patient and firm, on whatever stand she took. First thing to do, then, was win Pops over. Betsy found him sitting in his armchair, reading one of his thick volumes of history, one long leg hung over the other.

"Popsy, I'm sorry I was gone so long. Did you miss me?" She leaned against his shoulder.

He lowered his book. "We didn't get much done this morning, Bets. Your mother will not be pleased."

"You're not scared of Mother." She knew he wasn't. He didn't have to be. Even when Mother was mad at him, she treated him as if he were breakable.

"I'm not, am I?" he asked quizzically.

"No. She won't yell at you."

"She doesn't have to yell. She's a woman who needs only to look."

"Mmmm," Betsy agreed. She knew just what he meant. Mother could make you feel guilty or proud or anything just by putting her eyes on you in a certain way. "Maybe we should do some more boxes, then."

"I suppose we should. It wouldn't hurt Hal to do a few, too, the lazy lout. He claimed willingness. Trouble is, he's at that supremely selfish stage of life when his own interests are all that matter to him."

"He's looking for a job. Maybe he can't find one."

"Well, then he can go looking some other time, can't he?"

"He has to go to school tomorrow, Pops."

"So he does, but he'll have time after. How come you feel the need to defend him, Bets? Think I'm not fair to your poor brother? Think I'm not doing right by him?"

"I think you're wonderful, Pops. You know that."

He sighed. "You have admirable taste." He picked up his glass from the end table. His long tapered fingers were beautiful. Betsy had loved watching him play the piano. He could get as absorbed in playing as in reading. Once he had tried to teach her to play, but she learned too slowly to suit him. Then they'd had to sell the piano, anyway.

"Pops, I want to talk to you about something now while we're alone."

"Private business?"

"Sort of."

"A conspiracy?"

"What's a conspiracy?"

"You and me against everybody else."

"Yes," she said.

"Well, first find where your mother hid my carton of cigarettes."

"Then you'll listen to me?"

"Don't I always listen to you?"

"No," she said truthfully.

He sighed more deeply. "You mean I'm not a good father even to you, Betsy?"

"Of course you're a good father."

"I don't know," he brooded. "Maybe I'm not."

"You are a good father," she insisted, trying to keep his mood from slipping. She hurried to the kitchen. Boxes still cluttered the kitchen and dining room. Mother would be mad at them for sure. Betsy heard the front door open just as she located the fresh carton in the box marked *Miscellaneous*. She tensed. In the end, Mother was the one who would decide about Zoro. If only they'd unpacked more boxes!

"Helloool I'm home. Where are you, one and all?" Mother caroled cheerfully.

Betsy heard her father groan. "Don't shout, Moira. This is not an opera house. It is a small prison in which the inmates are used to long hours of deadly quiet."

"Where did the kids go?" Mother asked.

"Your son has been gone since breakfast. Your daughter's about, and I'm trying to relax. Do *not* expect me to unpack one more box of anything. I don't care if we live out of crates forever."

"Poor Lars. You always have hated domestic chores."

"Let's face it, Moira. I hate any chores. I'm basically a lazy bum. Why did you marry me?"

"Because you're so handsome."

Betsy returned to the living room. Her mother was sitting on the arm of her father's chair, kissing him. Mother looked up. Immediately her eyes went to the pack of cigarettes in Betsy's hand. Betsy could have kicked herself for not leaving it behind.

"I thought you said you'd try to cut down, Lars," Mother said.

"I felt I deserved some respite from my labors. Go look at all we unpacked."

Mother's dark, intelligent eyes assessed the stacks in the dining area instead. "Are those full or empty?"

"Those? Full, more than likely. It's your unfortunate compulsion to save every bit of our past lives, including cracked jars and aluminum foil throwaways. Do you know I counted thirty-five of those foil containers? What garbage do we eat from them?"

"Betsy, give your father his cigarettes and give me a kiss hello," Mother said, sidestepping her husband's complaint. "How was your day?"

"Well—" Betsy stalled, not sure this was the right time to begin pleading her case. She kissed her mother's cheek and ducked away from the searchlight eyes that had an uncanny way of seeing through her.

Sure enough, Mother asked, "Something troubling you, Betsy?"

"You won't believe what's out back," Betsy burst out.

"What?"

"There's a dog just waiting to *die* back there at the animal shelter. A wonderful dog. But we can save him. All you have to do is give me permission."

"Permission for what? What animal shelter?"

"Not animals again!" Her father groaned. "We just got here."

"Betsy, you were supposed to be helping your father unpack today," Mother said.

"I was helping. I was the only one helping. I did two boxes all by myself."

"What about Hal?"

"Hal went out looking for a job. He said he'd help tonight."

"All right," Mother said. "How about, after dinner, we all pitch in and unpack together?"

"No more," Pops groaned. "Moira, it will get done in time. Don't start nagging us to do it yesterday, please."

The subject of saving Zoro had somehow been mislaid. "Zoro wouldn't be any extra work for you," Betsy said.

"Who's Zoro?" her mother asked.

"He's a Doberman, a purebred Doberman over at the shelter, and they're going to kill him unless you let me adopt him."

"What are you talking about? Where is this shelter?"

"That building behind us past the barn? It's an animal shelter. They call it a shelter, but what it is really is a place where they murder poor animals that never did anything but love people and wag their tails and—"

"No," Mother interrupted, slapping her hands down on her thighs to check the flow of Betsy's words. "Permission denied."

"You couldn't have rented us a house near an animal shelter, Moira," Pops said incredulously. "You couldn't have been that careless. Do you forget Miss Harley's German shepherd and the way Betsy practically moved in with that dog? You know how hysterical she got when it died."

Mother shook her head. "I guess I didn't check out the location enough, after all. I couldn't have done much worse, could I? Betsy, I'm afraid the only thing we can do is forbid you to go near the place."

"But, Mother, he looked me in the eye, and it was just like mental telepathy. We understood each other right off. I love him, and he's such a great dog, and he never had a chance. You can't imagine what a life he's had. All you need to do is sign. You won't have to do a thing for him after that. You won't even know he's around. I'll take every bit of care of him myself. . . . Popsy?" She looked pleadingly from one to the other. Their faces were masks of resistance. "I never ask you for anything much. Can't I have just this one thing I want, just this time? I won't ever ask you for anything again, ever."

"Betsy, you know we'd like to let you have a dog, but we've discussed this subject I don't know how many times before. There's no way we can keep a dog in the house when your father's allergic to fur the way he is."

"The doctor said he could take shots."

"No, I will not take shots."

"You wouldn't even have to go near Zoro, Popsy. We'll keep him out in the backyard."

"The winters around here are too cold," Mother said.

"But it's spring. We could keep him until it gets cold and then—"

"And then what? Then we let him in the house and your father can't breathe like the last time when you sneaked that puppy into your bedroom."

"That wasn't my fault. How'd I know Pops was going to get sick?"

"This time you know," Mother said.

"They're going to kill him. Even if we just kept him until winter, that would be a few more months he'd have to live."

"And you'd get so attached to him, it would be twice as hard to give him up. No . . . Lars, say something to your daughter."

"Your mother knows best, as always," he said.

"Lars!" Moira said. "Can't you tell Betsy what you honestly think?"

"I think Zoro is a rotten name for a dog," he said.

"Besides," Mother said, giving up on her husband, "even if your father weren't allergic, we just can't afford to add any expenses right now. The idea is to try to cut back. We're making do with one salary instead of two. That means we have half as much to live on, Betsy."

"Money!" Betsy said bitterly. "Why is it always dollars and cents? Don't you think a dog's life is worth more than money? How much does a bag of dog food cost, anyway? I'll be happy to pay for his food out of my allowance."

Her mother bit her lip and stayed calm. Betsy could never understand how her mother stayed so calm all the time. "It's not just food," Mother said. "It's vet bills and licenses and—Betsy, I'm not going to go on arguing with you. It just isn't possible for you to have that dog." Mother forced a smile. "Why do I always come out of these discussions feeling like Mean Mama of the year? You make me feel cruel when I know very well I'm just being sensible."

"Your daughter," Pops said, "is one big feeling heart. What she lacks in intellect, she makes up for in emotion. Can you imagine what it's going to be like when it's boys instead of dogs she falls in love with?"

"I'll always love dogs," Betsy said. "Mother—"

"Betsy, please try to be practical. You're not a baby any more. You can't base all your actions on how you feel without considering the effects on others."

"If you let me get Zoro, he can have half of everything I eat. That way it won't cost you anything to keep him," Betsy said stubbornly, hearing only the pounding of her heart, knowing she was losing ground.

"Half of what you eat? Half of nothing is nothing. He'll starve to death."

Her father laughed.

Betsy couldn't stand it. Her heart was breaking and they found her amusing. "Could you just come and look at him?" she begged.

"What I don't understand," Pops said as if Betsy weren't there, "is how she could have stumbled on the place the instant she wandered out of the house. It's incredible bad luck, Moira. I suggest we repack and move immediately, some place closer to town. We're too far out in the boondocks here, anyway."

"Lars, I told you. This was the only place I could find that we could afford that wasn't a hovel. If you had come with me—"

"Ah, I knew we'd get to that—if *I* had come with you."

"I know you were too depressed, Lars. I'm just saying—"

"That I shouldn't have been. That I have no right to break down, being the man of the house, the paterfamilias, the—"

"Lars! Please. I picked the house. I'm sorry."

He inhaled his cigarette deeply, closed his eyes and began puffing out smoke rings. "I shall look for a better habitation as soon as I am up to it," he announced. "In the meantime, chain Betsy to her bed or she will be after us day and night. She'll never let us rest. She's the Joan of Arc of the canine set."

Mother laughed. "Lars, stop acting crazy."

"But I am crazy," he said.

Hal showed up when they were almost finished with dinner. "Anything left for me?" he asked, six feet of hollow trunk waiting to be filled.

"Help yourself," Mother said. "It's on the stove."

He emptied the contents of pots onto his plate without looking, and began shoveling stew and squash into his mouth mechanically. "Well, I found an after-school job," he said. "It doesn't pay a whole lot, but at least I'll be saving something toward college."

"If you can handle school and a job and do well at both, that's wonderful," Mother said.

"I can handle it. The only problem is, I don't see how I'm going to save enough in a year and a half."

"I told you we'd help."

"You have enough to do carrying the family on your shoulders as is, Mom."

Hal's remark was aimed like a punch at their father, but all Pops said was, "We could have used your help today."

"I'll work tonight," Hal said. "Tomorrow I start school, and after school, I go right over to the hamburger stand. I work until eleven."

Betsy heard all the crosscurrents of accusation and defense through the fog of her discouragement. She was trying to think of another approach to her mother, but as usual when she tried to solve a problem, no solution came. All she could do was barge ahead and try whatever came to her as she went along.

After dinner Hal tackled the unpacking with his usual energy, and Pops silently toted empty boxes stuffed with the newspaper that had been used to wrap things out to the garage. Betsy was washing the seldom-used good dishes while her mother dried them and stowed them away in the kitchen cabinets.

"Mother," Betsy said. "Was there ever something in your life you just had to have, something you wanted so badly you thought you'd die if you didn't get it?"

Mother thought a minute and then she said, "There was a boy I felt that way about."

"And what did you do?"

"I suffered."

"Mother, you've got to let me save Zoro. You've got to."

Her mother gave her a sympathetic look. "Do you remember that puppy? You suffered over him, too. You've got to stop breaking your heart over all the poor dogs in the world—and cats and gerbils and guinea pigs. Now if you want to keep a snake or a turtle. . . . Couldn't you manage to get attached to a lizard somehow?"

"Zoro's not just any dog. At least come with me and see him. Would you do that at least?"

"No, I'm tired. I've had a long day at a demanding job, and now there's all this unpacking still to do and work I brought home I should look at, besides. I just am not able to put myself through any more. I can't."

"You can do anything if it's for Pops or Hal, but nothing I want is important. I don't count for anything in this family," Betsy said, too upset to care how tired her mother was.

"Whining won't help, Betsy. I explained the reality of the situation to you once. You're not dumb and you did understand me."

Betsy's tears fell silently into the wash water as she worked. The reality of the situation was that they treated her like a baby, and what could a helpless baby do to save Zoro? She brooded while she went on rinsing off plates and stacking them in the dish holder for her mother to dry and put away.

Zoro, she thought before she fell asleep, and in her dream she opened his cage and he flew out as a huge brown bird, carrying her with him up into a black, endless night.

Chapter Four

What Betsy awoke with was the realization that she had to face a new school today.

"You'll make friends easily there, Betsy," her mother had promised her. "Lots of after-school activities for eighth-graders and a late bus to take you home."

It had sounded good. A new school meant a fresh start where nobody thought of her as the skinny little nothing who'd been such a crybaby in first grade. She could pretend to be the daring kind of girl she wanted to be. She wasn't ready, though. She needed more time to psych herself up for making the right first impression. Besides, she still had to plan how to get Zoro out of the shelter. Too much pressure always made her feel sick to her stomach. The tide of nausea was already rising in her. She padded off to the kitchen in her shorty nightgown to complain, "Mother, I'm sick."

Her mother understood her too well. "Come on, Betsy. You're O.K. It won't do any good to delay going. The longer you delay, the more scared you'll be. It's like cold water. The best way is just to plunge in."

"The best way with cold water," Pops said, "is to avoid it or wait for it to warm up."

"Lars, don't encourage her. She has to go to school."

"But she does look pale, Moira. Didn't you sleep well last night, baby?"

Drawn by his sympathy, Betsy trailed over and dropped her head languidly onto his shoulder. "I really do feel rotten. How can I make a good impression if I feel like I'm going to throw up in people's faces?"

"Go lean on your mother's shoulder if you're going to throw up," her father said heartlessly and went on drinking his coffee while he read the comics, the only part of the local paper he had declared worth reading.

"Come here and let me feel your head," Mother said. "Does anyone know where the thermometer is?"

Hal was gulping some kind of banana and yogurt milkshake he had made himself in the blender. Pops didn't deign to answer. Betsy said, "I think it got broke."

"Got broken—what am I saying—was broken,"

Mother said. "Maybe you do feel a little feverish. Oh, my God! Look at the time. I'm going to be late. All right, look, you can stay in bed, then. But Bets, you may not—I repeat—*not* go near that shelter. And try not to spend the whole day in front of the television set. Read that book you got for Christmas. O.K.?"

"Don't worry, Mother. You have a good day, and thanks." Betsy kissed her good-by.

"I have a feeling I've just been took," Mother said. "Lars, are you going to be around today?"

"Since we only have one car, I don't believe I have much choice."

"Well, there is the motorbike."

"I'm using that, Mom. Dad said it was O.K.," Hal said.

"It's all right. I plan to spend the day researching some avenues of employment, maybe working on that article on education I want to write."

"Oh, good, Lars. That's one where you really have a lot to say."

"I always have a lot to say. The question is, who wants to listen?"

"Do it, Lars. I'm sure you'll find an audience once you have it done."

"I don't need to be encouraged like one of the kids, Moira. But thanks, anyway."

His good humor was hanging by a thread. Betsy held her breath hoping her mother would have the sense to shut up. Mother's big mistake was always trying to organize their lives. It had

gotten so that all she had to do was start.
Whoever she started on steeled himself to resist
even if what she said was right. They'd be better
off if she let them all be. Finally she left in a flurry
of instructions about the telephone hook-up and
the garbage-collection service.

Betsy started thinking about school. She had
seen the campus of sprawling brick buildings that
included elementary, middle and high school, too.
Kids swarmed off a fleet of yellow school buses
from all over the district. How was she going to
find a friend in that beehive? She'd never even be
noticed. But imagine if she could be! Imagine if she
came on so cool, so winning that she walked right
into the heart of an in-group. Hal said she was a
natural-born actress. How did a winner act? She
wasn't sure. Maybe if she dressed for the part.
But what did she have to wear? She had until tomorrow to decide that. In the meantime, she'd go
see how Zoro was doing. What her mother had
said about not going near the animal shelter was
too unreasonable to be taken seriously.

"I'm going back to bed, Pops," she told her father, crossing her fingers and hoping he wouldn't
decide to come check on her.

She dressed in jeans and a sweater and climbed
out her bedroom window. A chilly rain drizzled
from a rumpled gray sky. The ground was muddy
where the grass had worn away. The barn looked
forlorn in the rain. She ran past it, eager to see
Zoro again. No dogs in the outside cages. She

panicked, imagining they had all been killed. Then she realized the dogs were probably kept inside in weather like this. She stepped through the open back door of the shelter and hesitated. She heard the *screek* of a cage opening and the yipping of a small dog. To her left in the corridor was a gray metal door that said *Keep Out*. She pulled it open and looked into a strange chamber. A cat lay on the raised floor, not moving. Nothing else in the stark space. Nothing but the discolored walls, a bare light bulb and an open pipe. She sniffed—some kind of disinfectant. All at once she closed the door and leaned against it, trembling. The cat must be dead. This must be the death chamber. Zoro! Never! Never him. She would steal him and run away from home with him first.

Shivering, she walked around to the center corridor that passed between the inside cages. The tall, thin Chinese boy was ladling out dry dog chow from a large bag into metal dishes, one to a cage. "You back again?" he said when he looked up and saw her.

"Uh huh. Is Zoro O.K.?"

"Go see for yourself. He nearly took my hand off when I gave him his breakfast. Doesn't give any warning, just lunges at you. You sure know how to pick your friends."

"And what about the golden retriever that came in yesterday, Sheila?"

"She got adopted last night before we even got a card made out on her."

"Good." She smiled. "My name's Betsy. What's yours?"

"Bill Wing."

"Willie Wing. That's like a nursery rhyme. Do kids ever tease you?"

"You call me Willie and I'll lock you in a cage with Zoro."

"That's no threat. He wouldn't bite me."

"So you say."

"He's a good dog, really."

"Your folks say you can adopt him?"

"Yes," she lied easily. "It's going to take them a while to get here, though. They're busy with moving in and everything."

"How come you aren't helping?"

"I just came by to see Zoro. I live back there." She pointed.

He nodded. "Well, I've got work to do, Betsy."

"There's no problem, is there?"

"In what?"

"In leaving Zoro here until we're settled and can take him home. I mean, you're not going to do anything to him right away?"

"He's got time."

"I saw that room."

"What room?"

"Where the dead cat is. That's where you do it, isn't it?"

"You shouldn't have looked in there."

"I don't see how you can do that. Take an animal and just kill it—just—you look like a nice person. I don't see how you can stand doing a thing like that."

"Well, I don't like that part of the job. I don't like a lot of parts of this job. Cleaning out cages, especially if an animal is sick and has the runs, is pretty disgusting. And putting them down—Listen, I used to go out in the garage to cry every time. The pay isn't much, either—minimum wage. I could make a decent living if I was working in my uncle's restaurant instead."

"Then why do you do it?"

"Because—because—it's a long story, and it's none of your business, anyway."

"Do you really cry?"

He took a deep breath. She could see he was sorry he had let that slip. "Not any more," he said. "Only the first few times. I still hate to do it, though, even though the carbon monoxide gets filtered through water so it doesn't burn their lungs and they really don't feel a thing. But—"

"But they know they're going to die."

"Yeah, I think so. Sometimes they just look up at you, and it makes you feel so rotten, or they'll whimper. I don't know how much longer I'm going to stick it. The thing is, I like Mr. Berrier. He's a decent guy—fair, and you can talk to him. He understands about my dropping out of school and all."

"You dropped out of school?"

"I'm sixteen."

"So?"

"So I'm not the greatest student in the world."

"Me, either. I stink. But I'm not planning to be a high school dropout."

"Yeah, well . . ." He hesitated over further confidences, then said, "Like I said, I've got work to do."

"I'm fifteen," she told him, surprising herself with this lie.

"You are?" He sounded incredulous.

"You thought I was younger. It's because I'm slender."

"Slender, huh?" He grinned.

She tilted her chin up, daring him to make it "skinny." Instead, he said, "How come you're not in school?"

"I'll be going soon. Maybe sometime you could tell me why you dropped out. I'll bet you're not that bad a student. It's not so hard to get C's here, is it?"

"C's isn't good enough," he said.

"For who?"

"You sure are a nosy kid." But he was smiling.

"I'm just interested in you."

"How come?"

"I guess I like you—sort of," she said loftily and held her breath in case he began to make fun of her now that she'd given him an opening.

"Do you?" he asked. "Well, you sure are a crazy kid, and you sure don't look fifteen."

She smiled and tried to raise her eyebrow in the way her mother did that looked so cool. She wanted him to like her. Besides, she might need him to help her save Zoro once she had a plan figured out.

"I think I'll go say hello to my dog now," she said.

"You really shouldn't be here this early."

"I'm not going to disturb anything, Bill. Please!"

He sighed. "Go ahead, but stay outside his cage and be careful you don't get bit. You hear?"

He was cute, she thought. He was open and easy to get around and she liked his looks. She flipped her hair back over her shoulders and swung her hips as sexily as she could, walking down the aisle to Zoro's cage.

The dog stood up when he saw her, silent but aware. She crouched in front of his cage, holding onto the bars, and called to him softly. His stump of a tail wagged tentatively.

"Here, boy. Come say hello. Here, boy. How are you today? Come say hello to me, Zoro . . . Zoro."

There was nothing soft or cuddly about him. He stood alert and powerful, a prince of dogs. His nobility set him apart, so did eyes so full of painful experience they made her sad just to look at him. "Zoro," she entreated, and slowly he stepped toward her. "My parents wouldn't let me adopt you, but don't you worry. I'll find a way to save you. I'll make Bill help us. Don't you worry." She put her face to the bars and blew him a kiss.

"Hey, you! Get away from that cage before you get hurt."

She started backward at the rumble of the man's voice. Immediately Zoro began to bark. His bark was staccato and deep. The man, Mr. Berrier, took a step toward the cage and Zoro turned violent. He threw himself at the bars on his side, bounced off and threw himself again. Betsy could feel the bruising in her own body. "Stop it! Stop that, Zoro!" she screamed. "It's all right. That man's not going to hurt us." But the dog wouldn't listen to her, and his violence turned into frenzy as the man came closer. Again and again he lunged at the bars with his jaws snapping and his upper lip drawn back over shark-like teeth.

"I told you that dog's a killer. I told you yesterday. How'd you get in here, anyways? I didn't see you come in this morning," Mr. Berrier said angrily.

"Mr. Berrier, don't be mad, please. I just came to see him. He is my dog, after all."

"Him? He's no good. I told you that."

"You said I could have him if my parents said it was O.K."

He shook his head. Zoro was settling down, growling, menacing, but he had stopped jumping. A blood streak crossed his face. "Look at that beast. Use your head, honey. He's too scared of people to make a pet out of him."

"But he likes me. I'll show you." She made a move toward the latch on the cage. Mr. Berrier grabbed her arm. Zoro went mad again until Mr. Berrier backed off up the aisle, leaving Betsy to stand there. Gradually, the dog calmed down, but his hysteria had set off the other dogs who yowled or barked or howled like mad prisoners in a jail.

"Look what you started here now," Mr. Berrier said.

"I'm sorry. I didn't mean to. It was all right until you came."

"Now, listen," Mr. Berrier said. "You look around and find youself another dog, but not now. Come back with your folks later when we open after one. I don't want you hanging around now. We can't have you upsetting the whole place like this. We got work to do here."

"You said I could adopt Zoro if I got my parents' permission," Betsy complained, her voice high-pitched with misery.

"I know what I said. What I thought was your folks would talk some sense into you once they saw what it was you wanted. Look, you want him to bite your mother or your brothers and sisters and friends who come to visit? That dog can't be trusted with people. Suppose you were out in the yard and somebody knocked into you for fun or by accident? He'd tear out their throat before you could stop him."

"I could tame him. I could train him to love people."

"I'm not going to waste my breath arguing with you." He turned on his heel. The Pomeranian with the feathered hoop of a tail appeared in the corridor and trotted up to him. Mr. Berrier said, "Want to go out, Winston? Come on, then."

Betsy trailed after him miserably. "It's not fair," she said. "You said Winston bit people. And you made him a mascot. Why should he get a chance and not Zoro?"

"Because Winston—" Mr. Berrier stopped in his tracks to think it over. He picked up the Pomeranian, holding the dog in the crook of his arm while he thought. "Winston doesn't go after people. He just doesn't trust strangers, and he won't bite a stranger if the stranger doesn't try to touch him. But you take that Doberman, he starts growling if you get near him. We'll be lucky if we don't get sued from one fellow came in here looking for a guard dog for his lumber yard. All he did was put his hand out for the dog to sniff, and that dog sank his teeth in the fellow's arm."

"Zoro probably thought the man was going to hit him."

"What's the difference what he thought? He's a mean dog."

"You're going to kill him?"

"Have to, eventually."

"What are you waiting for, then?"

"I like to hold them as long as I can."

"Why?" If there was a softness in him, she needed to find it.

"Oh, why—because sometimes at the last minute the ones you least expect to will get lucky. We had a dog in here, old fellow, getting gray around the muzzle. All he did was lie around the cage all day quiet. He didn't even wag his tail when a kid came in looking for a pet. It was like he knew there wasn't any use in competing. Then one day in comes an old guy wanted a quiet dog to keep him company. He took one look at that sad-looking mutt and said, 'He's the one.' The way he figured was they both only had a little time left."

Good, she thought. Mr. Berrier believed in fate and welcomed miracles, then. She put her hand on his arm. "Please don't put down Zoro. I'm sure he's going to get lucky."

"I can't promise you anything, honey. When the cages get crowded, we got to make room somehow, and the ones who've been here longest—"

"But he has weeks yet, doesn't he?"

"No way of telling. Sometimes the place is pretty empty for months, and other times they pile up here like flies on a sugar spill. We're full now."

"Maybe I could help out," she said.

"Doing what?"

"There must be something I could do. I love animals. I'd do anything."

"No," Mr. Berrier said. "We don't need any volunteers. You want to look around at the other dogs, though, you can. Just don't hang around Zoro . . . Say, shouldn't a kid your age be in school?"

"We just moved in. I start soon." She remembered she had told him she was thirteen. She hoped he didn't talk to Bill about her.

"O.K.," he said. "Just don't cause me any more trouble in here." He tried to look severe, but his weathered face registered kindness no matter how he frowned.

"Mr. Berrier," Bill said, stepping into the corridor. "That collie they brought in yesterday looks bad."

"O.K., Bill. I'll take a look at her. Maybe we'll send her over to the vet."

"Bill," she said when Mr. Berrier had gone, "I could clean up the dog doo for you if you want."

"What for?"

"You said you hate it."

"Wouldn't you mind doing that kind of stuff?"

She did mind, but she thought she could get used to it, and she wanted to have an excuse for spending a lot of time at the shelter. It would take a lot of time to change Zoro's personality. "I just want to help any way I can."

"No," he said, "I'd feel funny letting you clean cages. Like I was shirking my job or something. Tell you what, you can hose them down if you want. I'm going to put the dogs outside now. I have to take their dishes out and clean the cages and rinse the bowls with a germicidal solution. We do that to cut down on the respiratory disease they get after they've been here a while."

"What respiratory disease?"

"It's kind of a cough they get—kennel cough, Mr. Berrier calls it. The cats die from it in a week sometimes."

"But that's awful! People shouldn't bring their animals here."

"Yeah, well, we handle maybe six thousand animals a year here and almost half of those have to be put down. It could be worse. If this wasn't a privately funded shelter, we'd have to let animals go to be used in experimental labs."

She shuddered and swallowed. "It makes me sick," she said. "It makes me just sick." She wondered what would happen if some night she sneaked in here and opened all the cages and let the dogs and cats loose to take their chances. Sometimes people took in stray animals that appeared in their yards. It could happen, and they'd be better off foraging for themselves than being stuck in cages waiting their turn for the gas chamber.

"Is this place locked up at night?" she asked casually.

"No, just the front door, usually. An old guy lives in an apartment off the office there. He's the night watchman. Somebody has to be on call, see, even at night, in case of an emergency."

"And the dogs are inside at night?"

"Yeah— Hey, Betsy, don't start getting any ideas. You can't just come in and turn that dog loose, you know. Suppose he killed somebody, a little kid maybe—how'd you feel?"

"I wasn't going to turn him loose." Not *just* Zoro—she'd been thinking of all the animals.

"Good. It would be a stupid idea. You know what? I want you to see that collie Mr. Berrier's looking at."

"Why?"

"Because she's a stray, been on her own for a good while."

"How can you tell?"

"You'll see when you look at her."

Bill let her hose down the cages after he sent the animals outside and shoveled out their droppings. She liked working alongside him. He was quick, cheerful and kind to the animals. She even began adjusting to the smells. "Do you have a girlfriend, Bill?" she asked idly.

"Now what kind of question is that? Sure I have girlfriends."

"Not just one, though."

"No. And that's all the personal questions I'm going to answer."

"You can ask *me* something if you like."

"What?" He looked confused as if she had embarrassed him.

"What do you want to know?"

"O.K. Tell me this. Did your parents really say you could have Zoro?"

"Not actually in so many words."

"You were lying, huh?"

"It wasn't a lie exactly. I just haven't convinced them yet—not all the way, but I will."

"You're too much."

"But you like me?" she asked, her confidence balancing precariously on his answer.

"You're not really fifteen, either."

She considered. "How old do you think I am?"

"How should I know? Twelve?"

"I'm older than you think, anyway."

"And you're the worst liar I ever met. I can't believe how you lie."

She sulked, letting him see how insulted she was, but he didn't react to the sulking, so she dropped it and said seriously, "You know what they ought to do is put people in jail for abandoning their pets."

"Right, fill up the jails with people whose landlords won't let them keep a dog. That's going to help a lot."

"Well, something ought to be done."

"The question is what?" Bill said. "I've thought about it a lot and I don't have any solutions. Of course, according to my father, I'm too dumb to think. So it's not surprising if I can't come up with anything."

"Your father really thinks you're dumb?"

"My father thinks anybody who isn't at the top of his class and who isn't a future candidate for Harvard Medical School is too dumb to be his son. My father thinks I'm just a spoiled, lazy kid."

"You're not lazy."

"Well, I'm not the hardest working student in

the world. I like to have a little time to fool around, at least."

"Just like me. Did you get passing grades?"

"B's mostly."

"B's!" She was indignant. "And you quit school? You should go back."

He laughed. "For a little kid who lies so much, you sure are bossy."

"Me bossy?" Again he had hurt her feelings. It was her mother who was bossy. She had never thought of herself that way. And just when she was about to tell him how much they had in common!

When the cages were clean and the dogs were all outside, Bill took her to the garage to show her the sick collie. The collie was lying on her side in a pen, too weak to move. Her eyes were crusted with sores, patches of hair gone from her back and sides and the rest matted solid. Bill said Mr. Berrier hadn't expected the dog to last the night, she was so starved. An old wound where she had been hit by a car seemed to be giving her pain. Still, she had eaten and drunk a little water.

"That's what happens to them when they're on their own," Bill said. "Either it's this or they turn wild and run in packs and attack chickens or sheep or little kids. Dogs and cats don't survive too well on their own."

"But Mr. Berrier will take her to the vet, won't he?"

"Sure," Bill said. "But it's probably pretty hopeless."

She was too choked up to talk any more. On her way home she stopped at Zoro's outside cage and called to him. The beagle in the cage next door barked for her attention She petted the two animals at the same time. It struck her that these dogs didn't get petted, not even touched by human hands, usually. Their keepers sent them back and forth between the inner and outer cages by pulling on a rope that raised the inside doors. Human prisoners had exercise yards, at least, and jobs to keep them occupied. The outside cage had a latched door, too, she noticed. She stopped patting the dogs and set to opening Zoro's cage.

When she stepped inside it, he backed away from her and cowered in a corner as far from her as he could get. "Here, baby, here," she whispered, holding out her hand to him, fist closed for him to come and sniff. He stood there watching her with his head down as if uneasy at her presence in his cage.

"Come on. You know I'm not going to hurt you," she said. She sat down and patted the concrete floor beside her. "Come here, Zoro." Stealthily the dog crept toward her, not wagging his tail this time. For an instant she was afraid. His head was on a level with her own, but she held steady while his moist black nose investigated her hand. Once he finally licked her hand, she relaxed.

"Zoro," she crooned and ran her hand lovingly over his head. The lightning streak of blood from the bars of the cage had dried now. He drew closer, leaned against her while she stroked him. She wondered if he'd ever been petted before. As a puppy, maybe? He whined softly and sat down with his body up against her leg. Then he lay his head in her lap.

"My dog," she whispered. "My Zoro."

Bill Wing's voice made her turn and look over her shoulder. "You really are crazy!" he said.

"I told you he liked me." Zoro growled low in his throat. "No, Zoro. Don't growl at him. He's a friend. He's going to help us."

"I am?" Bill asked.

"Sure you are," Betsy said. She felt Zoro's growing tension. He would start trying to break down the bars of the cage again soon if she didn't do something. "Bill, go away, please. I'll get out of the cage and go home when you're gone."

"But he might attack you."

"He won't hurt me."

Reluctantly he backed out of sight around the corner into the building. She patted the dog a few more times, and then reached through the bars and up to unlatch the cage and let herself out. "Stay," she told Zoro. "Stay. I'll be back as soon as I can to get you out of here."

Zoro watched her leave as if he had understood. She looked back once to see him staring after. Then she headed toward the barn. The barn!

She stopped in her tracks. If she couldn't keep Zoro in her own house, maybe she could keep him in the barn. Was it empty? She ran over to work at that stuck latch.

Chapter Five

Mother never let her stay home a second day without at least a low fever as proof of illness, and last night she had said pointedly, "The thermometer is found, Betsy." Today, then, she had to go to school. Even though she woke with her stomach clamped shut with anxiety, she had to go.

She began the long process of transforming herself into prettiness at six A.M. when she had the bathroom to herself. First the weedy hair had to be washed and treated with conditioner, then washed again and blown dry into a semblance of style. Never mind that the stylish look always disappeared the instant she turned her back on the mirror. This time might be different.

This morning she couldn't get the curls to angle right. The more she tried the worse it got. Finally, she dried the shine right out. Then Hal began hammering on the bathroom door, yelling at her to get out. She gave up and scooted past him to see about disguising her body instead.

"There should be a timer on this bathroom door so people who don't have consideration for others get their eardrums blasted when they stay in too long," Hal shouted after her.

She forgot the padded bra and had to pull off the red shirt and start again. Saggy-haired was bad enough without looking flat-chested, too. Even with the padding, all the mirror reflected was an undernourished ten-year-old with anxious eyes. How could she make an impression the way she looked? She tried on the red, high-heeled sandals she had bought on an impulse with her birthday money. There, that was better.

Her mother was already gone when Betsy slipped into the kitchen for a glass of milk. No sign of her father. Hal had the morning paper all to himself. He looked up from it to say, "What are you dressed up as?"

"I'm going to school."

"That way?"

"Don't I look nice?"

"You look ridiculous."

She turned her back on him. "Just because you couldn't get in the bathroom, do you have to be so mean?" she asked, not letting him see her quivering lip.

"I'm not being mean. I'm telling you the truth. Those shoes make you look ridiculous."

"A lot you know."

"O.K., don't listen to me, then."

"Lots of girls wear heels."

"Not kids your age."

She considered. He was right about that. But the shoes gave her courage. They projected an image of glamour. "I'm going to wear them anyway," she said.

"Suit yourself." He went back to his paper.

She looked at her shoes doubtfully. If she took them off, she'd be nothing. Nobody would even notice her. She would walk through that huge complex of buildings all alone and anonymous. She'd take a chance on the shoes. "Hal?" she said.

"Uh?"

"You know that barn at the back of the yard? Who does it belong to?"

"How should I know? You been in it?"

"No. The door's hard to open. It's not our barn, though?"

"I don't think so. Why are you interested?"

"I'm not. I just asked."

Pops shambled into the kitchen yawning. "I was instructed to see to it you got to school this morning, Bets. I see you've managed to start by yourself. How're you feeling?"

"Awful."

"Good, good. You're back to normal, then. Well,

get cracking, girl. Don't stand there wilting all over the floor."

"Do I look O.K., Pops?"

"No worse than usual." He yawned, his eyes barely open, not interested in how she looked.

"Do you want me to take you to the guidance office in the middle school?" Hal asked. "That's where you've got to check in."

"No, thanks," Betsy said. She tilted her chin up. "They're expecting me, after all."

She made the bus by taking her shoes off and running for it barefoot. Kids stared at her all right, but nobody said anything. She took the seat right behind the driver so she wouldn't have to look at anybody, and she fitted her shoes back on. Most of the way to school, she sat staring out the window. They passed an empty store with a For Sale sign in its dirty front window. *Jack's Appliances,* the sign still read. Was that the store where Zoro had lived? She bet it was. How many other appliance stores had gone out of business on Blue Barns Road?

The middle school had long, bare corridors with washable walls and echoing floors. The unfamiliar faces passed her, scaring her more by the minute. But when she had been processed through guidance and deposited in a first-period math class, she found they were using the same math book she'd just managed to pass in Brooklyn. That meant her worst subject would be a greased slide. Then it turned out her social studies teacher was a cute young man, definitely an improvement over the tyrant she had left behind. Optimism began perking through her fears.

She crossed her legs and swung her red-sandaled foot to attract attention. Except for one boy who snickered, no one said anything to her, not until health, which was the period just before lunch. She sat watching other kids wrap each other up in splints and bandages, thinking if the shoes weren't enough, maybe she would bring in a pack of cigarettes and try smoking them in class tomorrow. That would get their attention, and maybe the teachers could be convinced smoking in class was accepted practice in Brooklyn. So what if she ended up getting punished?

A hand touched her shoulder. "Next period's lunch," a slightly buck-toothed girl with a sunny face said. "If you'd like to sit with my friends and me, just head toward the window. We always sit at a table next to the third window."

"Why, thanks!" Betsy said gladly.

As she approached their table with her tray in her hands, she looked them over. Not a boy anywhere near them. Girl Scout uniforms on two of the girls. Another girl was very fat and one had weirdly crossed eyes, not at all the type of girls she had hoped to find. Her luck to be picked up by the lame ducks instead of an in-group. She considered walking right on past them. It would be a mistake to risk identification with a group of losers. The red shoes should do better for her than that. But she stopped at the table and said to the sunny-faced girl, who looked pretty enough when her mouth was shut, "You don't have room enough for me. I'll sit somewhere else. Thanks, anyway."

"No, no," the girl said, smiling toothily. "I saved you a seat next to me." She unpiled a load of books from the chair beside her and began introductions before Betsy could think of another excuse. To her surprise, she found the group interesting. They were absorbed in quizzing one of the Girl Scouts on her reasons for wanting to become a Mormon. Betsy was impressed with the girl's intelligent answers. Next it turned out that Karen, the sunny-faced girl, had a boyfriend, an older boy from Karen's neighborhood. He had a driving permit. Not even the red shoes could compete with that.

"I have a boyfriend, too," Betsy said. "He works at the animal shelter. He's sixteen."

"Oh, really?" Karen said. "Isn't that nice." And the notion that Betsy had a boyfriend made an instant bond between them.

"Do you like my shoes, Karen?" Betsy asked later in the girls' room.

"Shoes? Oh, I didn't notice them before. They're really pretty. Are they your mother's?"

"No." Betsy was stung by the question. "They're my own."

"Oh," Karen said cheerfully. "I should have guessed. You walk so good in them."

It turned out that each of the girls lived in a different out-of-the-way neighborhood in the spread-out school district. All they seemed to have in common was a need to belong, a sheeplike instinct to herd together against the lonely spaces of the big school complex. Betsy was willing to be part of the herd so long as they accepted her as she was, uncritically. They weren't an in-group, but they were a group at least. Later that day, in physical science, the girl who wanted to be a Mormon took Betsy as a partner and helped her through the bewildering processes. Then the cross-eyed girl greeted her by name in the hall. Little things, but they made Betsy feel comfortable in the new school.

She pranced off to the bus that afternoon head up, walking well. Somewhere she had read that a woman who walks well always looks beautiful.

"So how did it go?" her mother asked her that evening.

"Not bad."

"Really? Not bad? That's terrific," Mother teased. "Want to give me the details?"

"Mother, I wish you wouldn't make fun of me. Why does everybody in this whole family always poke fun at me?"

"I wasn't making fun of you, love. I am just sincerely glad it turned out better than you expected."

She was pacified and would have given her

mother a minute-by-minute description of her day if her father hadn't interrupted them.

"Moira, we seem to be out of beer."

"Are we? Well, Saturday when we go food shopping—"

"You can't possibly expect me to last until Saturday with no beer in the house and no cigarettes either."

"Whyn't you go out and buy some, Dad?" Hal asked, though he obviously knew the answer.

"Because at the moment I am without either cash or means of transportation, Hal. I say 'at the moment,' you notice? Now where's the shame in that?"

"I didn't say there was any shame in it," Hal said.

"Didn't you? Moira, why haven't you asked me how the job interview went?"

"I thought you would tell me when you were ready, Lars."

"Well, it went badly. You can tell your counselor friend that wasn't much of a lead he gave you. They weren't looking for a teacher or at least not an experienced teacher or at least not right now they're not looking, and in any case they didn't want me."

"Then it probably wasn't right for you. No loss," Mother said briskly. "It's just a matter of looking until the right one turns up."

"If it ever does," Pops said.

"Would you like to go for a walk with me, Lars?"

Mother was suggesting he might want to be alone with her to confess all his worries, Betsy knew. She felt a twinge of jealousy, but Pops said, "No, what I'd like to have is a beer or a cigarette at least."

"And how was your day, Mother?" Hal asked suddenly.

"Fine," she said. "I like my new job." She was signaling something to Hal with her eyes, but Betsy couldn't read that message. Hal could. He flushed and looked at his father and then away.

Mother and Hal had long private conversations with each other that stopped when Betsy came into the room. She wondered if he'd answer if she asked him why he didn't respect Pops. Just because Pops was out of work didn't make him a failure, did it? And why was Hal so mad at Pops for letting Mother do all the work? She did do most of the work, but she didn't seem to mind, and if Hal was so mad about it, why didn't he help more?

There was a time when Betsy could have talked like that with her brother. Hal used to carry her around on his back when she was little, and he'd been the one to hold her two-wheeler up when she was learning to ride. But he had always wanted money for wheels, money for college, money to invest in schemes to make more money. Last year she had gone door to door selling roasted-nut mix he'd cooked up at home and packed in old mayonnaise jars. She'd done all right, too, until she dropped the box. He claimed the broken jars had wiped out his profit, and he'd been so angry that he hadn't spoken to her for a week, as if she had deliberately ruined his business.

"What are you lost in thought about, Betsy baby?" Pops asked.

"Me? Nothing," Betsy said and turned to leave the room, dragging a sudden sadness with her. In her bedroom she lay down and thought of Zoro. She could feel his eyes focusing on her as if she were his whole world. Right now he was sitting in his cage, waiting. "Zoro," she whispered and thought of the barn. Thought pushed her into action. In a second she was out the back window again.

The barn had probably once been the center of a farm which had been sold off and made into lots along both Blue Barns Road and the lane on which Betsy's house stood. The barn doors faced empty fields, weed-sown now. Anyone entering through those doors wouldn't be visible from either the shelter or the house. The only windows were on that side, too. As for the noises Zoro might make if he were hidden there, the background of animal noises from the shelter would cover them. The barn was the perfect hiding place. But first she had to loosen that stuck bar that held the door shut. She found a fist-sized rock to use as a hammer and went to work. For a long time, longer than it took for her arms to ache, Betsy pounded at the bar. She had just about given up when it gave way. The door squealed open on rusty hinges.

Inside, the dusky interior smelled of damp earth, musty hay and traces of animal dung, horses' probably. One side was fenced off and fitted with a wooden floor. Wisps of hay, barely visible in the faint light from the cobwebbed windows on either side of the door, suggested what had been stored in the fenced area. The beaten earth under the high rafters on the other side of the building was marked off by wooden stalls. A pile of splintered boards and broken harness tack in the back yielded a find of burlap bags. Betsy dragged these into the hayloft area to make a mattress for Zoro.

She wished the place were not so dark and dusty for him. Still, it was better than the death chamber in the shelter. She would try to get him outside at night for exercise. The immediate problem was how to get him out of the shelter without Mr. Berrier knowing. Bill would have to help her. First of all, he could buy the dog food if she gave him money for it, and then maybe she could convince him to tell Mr. Berrier a story that would serve as a cover for Zoro's escape, although she had a feeling it wasn't going to be easy to get Bill to tell a lie.

In the narrow path of wan sunlight slanting through the window, the pile of burlap looked like a dead animal. So gloomy in the barn. Zoro couldn't stay here too long. There were more problems to solve than she could begin to consider. The most important one was how to get Zoro away from the shelter.

Her mind wandered away from the task. What would Bill say if he knew she had told Karen he was her boyfriend? She hadn't expected to have a boyfriend so soon, but if Karen was going to have one, why shouldn't she? And Bill was an older boy. An older boy was better than some show-off eighth grader who competed to see who could belch the loudest or talk the dirtiest. Boys her age were either gross or babyish. They couldn't talk normally to a girl the way Bill talked to her. She wondered if he thought she was attractive. She wasn't pretty, but a girl didn't have to be pretty to be sexy. The red sandals might do it. He'd be surprised next time he saw her. She smiled to herself and stretched languorously in the stream of dancing dust motes.

Chapter Six

Betsy was surprised to see the moon through her uncurtained window when she opened her eyes. Usually she woke up to morning. Milky moonlight stained the darkness, and the sky was dark blue behind the two black trees that she could see. The barn looked like a chalky slate in need of an eraser. Zoro would be lying in his concrete-floored cage in the shelter. Did he sleep through the night? Not likely. He'd be alert to the sounds, hear other dogs yipping in their dreams, maybe hear the peeping of the million frogs as she was hearing them. A truck clattered by on a road somewhere. The night was warm and still.

Impulsively, she pulled on the clothes she had dropped on the floor and vaulted out the window. She detoured past the ghostly barn and crept up to the unlocked back door of the shelter, wondering what the old man who kept watch would do if he caught her trying to sneak in. He might think she was a thief. Out to steal what? Something in the office—not dogs nobody wanted. She hoped he didn't wake up.

She tiptoed inside. Now if only the dogs didn't make a fuss when they saw her. She walked past the ominous gray door of the gas chamber, then glided into the corridor between the cages. She looked back over her shoulder nervously but saw nothing in the murky dimness behind her. A dog whoofed softly and came to the front of his cage.

"Quiet," she told him. "It's just me."

Another dog whimpered and one scratched at the wires of his cage, watching her with his tail wagging. She would have liked to let him out. She would have liked to let them all out, but she had learned her lesson from the pathetic collie. Letting them loose was a bad gamble. Better to take a chance of being adopted here.

Zoro was waiting for her, ears at alert. She unlatched the cage door and called to him. He came hesitantly at first. Then, as if he were afraid she might change her mind, he rushed out.

"Stop, Zoro! Stay!" she hissed, afraid that now he was free he wouldn't listen to her. He halted halfway down the corridor and looked back at her.

She caught up to him and bent down to hold his head and rub behind his ears while she told him, "You're going to have to stay beside me now, Zoro. You can't run off when we get outside." She needed a rope or a leash or something. She remembered seeing several hanging up for sale in the waiting room. "Stay," she said to him. "You stay here now." But when she tiptoed to the small entryway where the leashes were, Zoro was right at her heels. She selected a collar and leash, trying to keep the chains from jingling, imagining she could hear the old man snoring, hoping he was still snoring. Every ping crashed through the quiet night. She breathed easier when they were finally outside.

Zoro stayed so close beside her she could have guided him with her hand on his head without the leash. His obedience pleased her. She ran to the barn, which seemed less scary with him beside her even though the moonlight failed to subdue the shadows.

Once inside, she sat with her arms around Zoro and told him, "What we've got to do now is get you used to staying in the barn. You'll have to be so quiet. It's not much of a place for you, but it's better than your cage. Right, Zoro? And I'll bring you food and come to visit you a lot, but you're going to have to stay in hiding here. If anyone finds you, they'll send you right back to the shelter, and if you bit anyone—Oh, Zoro! You better not bite anyone. All they can do to me is yell and ground me for a month or something, but they can *kill* you. Are you going to be quiet and wait patiently in here for me? Can you do that?"

He licked her face and rubbed the back of his head against her shoulder. She unhooked the leash so that he was free to explore. "Go look the place over," she told him and shoved him along, but he didn't seem interested in leaving her side. She sat leaning against a post, with his head resting on her leg, trying to think of how she would get him out of the shelter without making Mr. Berrier suspicious. She couldn't just take him out at night and leave the cage empty. Mr. Berrier knew who wanted Zoro. He could find out where she lived. Then she'd have him *and* her parents watching her, and between them they'd think of the barn or see her going to it. How then?

She only realized she had dozed off when she woke up, scared at first because she didn't know where she was. "Zoro," she called then, and more sharply, "Zoro!"

In a second he reappeared in front of her. He had done his exploring after all. Relieved at his return, she snapped the leash onto the collar. "We've got to go back now. But we'll do this again. Maybe tomorrow night, maybe every night until I can think of something."

She felt his fighting strength when he resisted going back into his cage. No way could she physically force him to do anything. Finally, she got into his cage and called to him. He came to her, head down, submitting reluctantly. She kissed him and told him what a good, wonderful dog he was. "I'll be back soon," she said.

The other dogs had gotten so used to her that none of them made a sound when she left. She hung the leash and collar back up in the entry- way and pushed herself home through invisible waves of darkness, yearning for her bed and sleep.

Halfway across the yard, she saw the light snap on in her bedroom. She could see her mother dart- ing about in her red nylon nightgown as if Betsy might be hiding somewhere in the room. Now she was in for it! If she didn't pop through the win- dow instantly, her mother would be on the phone to the police.

"Mother, I'm here!" she called before she had hopped onto the cinder blocks and heaved herself up onto the sill.

"Betsy!" Mother looked startled. "What on earth are you doing roaming around outside at this time of night?"

"Walking. Can you give me a hand up, please?"

Mother's hands were delicate, as small-boned and thin as Betsy's own, though she was a chunky woman, a solid, competent woman who could do everything that needed to be done. The delicacy of her mother's hand, which suggested the girl she had been, touched Betsy oddly.

"O.K." Her mother plunked herself onto Betsy's bed with one bare leg curled under her, ready to stay a while. "I'm listening. Tell me what's bothering you."

"Nothing."

"When nothing's bothering you, you sleep nights. What are you doing wandering around in the dark?"

"Just taking a walk, Mother. It's nice out."

"You used to be afraid of the dark."

"Well, I'm not a baby any more. Besides, you're the one who said it was safe in the country. You said one of the advantages about moving here was how safe it was going to be."

"Were you thinking about your father?"

"What about my father?" Betsy avoided her mother's beautiful, probing eyes. Why couldn't she have inherited her mother's eyes, at least?

"I know he's usually the one you go to, and right now he's not giving you much. Are you feeling out of things?"

"What things?"

Her mother studied her a while. "You do understand how hard it is for him, don't you? He's irritable because he has to fight against feeling guilty and work at believing in himself. Some days it takes all his energy just to do that. But he's a capable man, and he'll come out O.K.—once he decides what he wants to do with himself. We just have to stand fast and show our faith in him."

"I'm not worried about Pops. He can take care of himself," Betsy said.

"O.K. Then I guessed wrong. Are you in love, Betsy?"

"Me?" Betsy was astonished. How could her mother flip from thinking of her as a baby to imagining she was a woman?

"I wish you'd give me a clue," Mother said. "We haven't had a good talk in such a long time. I don't even know what you're thinking about these days."

"Just the usual."

Mother sighed and put on a smile to show there were no hard feelings. "All right. I won't bug you. Don't make a habit of midnight walks, though. Even if it is pretty safe around here, you shouldn't take chances."

Betsy smiled.

Her mother put her arm around her and drew her close to kiss her good night. Betsy felt the softness of her mother's naked body under the nightgown and was repelled as she never was when her father drew her close.

Her mother got up and was about to turn out the light and leave when Betsy asked, "If I wanted something more than anything I've ever wanted in my life, would you help me get it?"

"Sure, if I could and it was something that's good for you."

Betsy took a deep breath. "Mother, let me have Zoro. I'll keep him in the yard. You won't even know he's out there."

"Betsy! You're such a little kid still. How can

you let yourself get so emotionally involved with an animal? There are hundreds, thousands, of animals in need of a home. What good is saving one dog going to do?"

"He's not just any dog. Zoro and I—it was like love at first sight, Mother. I'm the only one he loves. He doesn't trust anybody else."

"Great! You want to keep a dog in the yard who doesn't like people. Comes winter when it's too cold for him to be outside, what do we do? Move out so he can move in, or take a chance he's going to take a chunk out of one of us?"

"Some dogs live outside all year."

"You're conning me, Betsy, and it's still no."

"I have to save him. Don't you understand at all, Mother? He loves me."

"We love you, too. You have to consider other people's needs. We've been through all this. You know we have."

"You hate me!" Betsy accused. "You think I'm ugly and dumb and babyish. Well, I can't help being the way I am." She threw herself face down on her bed in frustration.

Her mother tried to pat her back, but Betsy shoved her hand away. "I don't know how I manage to blow it," Mother said, talking to herself, "but I blow it every time I try."

When Betsy finally looked up, the light was still on, but her mother was gone. Zoro was still in the shelter, and she was no closer to a solution than she had been before. She hugged her pillow, trying to set her mind to work on a plan, but all she could think of was how angry her mother made her. Why? Mother did try to be nice. Sometimes Betsy hated herself for hating her. But something about Mother always got Betsy's back up. Something, something . . . Mother had it all her way.

Chapter Seven

Betsy tried on every combination of tops and pants that might make Bill look at her as a female. He was on duty this Saturday, so she had all day to arouse his interest. Her best feature, she knew, was her shapely legs. The temperature was down to forty according to the radio news station Hal was listening to—frost on the ground this late in April—but since shorts would show off her legs, she wore them. A loose shirt tucked into the shorts camouflaged her flat chest. She tried tying her hair up on top of her head, but in the red heels she looked too much like an ostrich. Instead, she let her hair float loose and wore a bracelet and her birthstone earrings. A touch of lip ice, a brush of mascara and she looked as old as she could. She considered whether to leave by the window or risk Hal's mockery by walking through the house all dolled up. Better to skip breakfast and not have her confidence cut down by any comments.

The day was polished sharp and crisp after the frost. Even the grass shone as she climbed out and walked carefully across the yard, trying to ignore the chill and hoping the goose bumps on her legs weren't going to show. She hadn't been over to the shelter during the day for a while, though she had sneaked Zoro out to the barn often enough at night.

Yesterday she had gone home with Karen on her school bus. Karen was really nice, the kind of girl who never says anything about another person unless she can say something good. Her time was filled, though, with her boyfriend and all kinds of church activities. Karen's family were pretty religious. Her father was a deacon. When Betsy had told them she was an atheist, they had looked a little shocked. She'd worried that maybe she had shut up the friendship right then, but just before Mother arrived to pick up Betsy, Karen had said, "Maybe we could go to the teen coffee house together, you and Bill and my Ken and me."

"Maybe," Betsy agreed. She tried not to say too much about Bill, but Karen imagined they had a lot in common because Betsy had an older boyfriend, too. Betsy had invented some stuff about what Bill said to her and about times they had spent together. If worse came to worst, she could always tell Karen that she had broken up with Bill. Karen wasn't the kind to ask Bill any questions if she ever met him. But it would be great if Betsy could have some real experience to tell Karen.

She skirted the back side of the barn, trying a short cut to the shelter. A tree root caught her left foot. She tripped but didn't fall. It hurt so much she hobbled right past the outside cages without stopping to greet Zoro. Inside the shelter, she sat down on the floor to examine her ankle. Just her luck to have Bill come along then and find her sitting cross-legged and inspecting her ankle like a little girl.

"Hi, Betsy. What are you doing up so early?"

She looked up at him, disappointed that her entrance had been spoiled. "I came to see you," she said in a very small voice, "but I twisted my ankle."

"No wonder. Look at the dumb shoes you're wearing."

"Dumb shoes!" she exclaimed. "These are beautiful."

"Those stilts?"

She stood up to show him he was wrong, ignoring the pain. "I can walk on them perfectly well. I'm a girl, after all."

He grinned.

"Are you laughing at me?" she demanded.

"Me? No. Why would I laugh at you?" But he was still grinning.

"What are you doing with that dog?" she asked crossly. He had a fat old dog on a leash.

His smile left and his face took on a pained expression. "This is Major," he said. Major, hearing his name, wagged his tail. His eyes were cloudy with cataracts and the grizzled hairs around his jaws and nose gave his age away. "We got two new dogs in last night," Bill said.

"So?" Betsy asked, even though she now knew perfectly well where he was heading with Major.

"So his time's come. I've got to put the poor old beggar down."

"You can't do such a thing," she said. "Look at him!"

"I told you that's part of my job," he said. "Don't make it worse for me, Betsy."

"But how can you go and kill him? He likes you. Look, he wants to be your friend. You couldn't be that mean."

"Betsy, come on. Stop it. You know how it is. Nobody's adopted him. He's too old and the family that owned him moved. He's part of the junk they left behind. You want to pick some other dog for me to put down today? Go ahead. Be my guest."

"You could take him home with you."

"You don't know where I live."

"Where do you live?"

He shrugged. "I don't want to talk about it. Just believe me, I couldn't keep a dog there, and besides, what am I supposed to do, fill the place with all the dogs that have to be put down? We did ten this week alone."

"How can you stand it? Why don't you do something? You know what we could do? We could go knock on people's doors until we find someone willing to take them. We could—"

"They're already advertised on TV. There's a local talk-show-lady in the morning who advertises two or three dogs and a cat a day for us. A lot of them get adopted that way."

"But the ones that don't get adopted—"

"I told you. I don't like this any better than you do, but it's part of my job."

"Then quit the job."

"What good's that? Somebody else would do it, and I need this job. It was hard enough to find. Everybody wants you to have a high school diploma. I was getting ready to go home and let my father chain me to the desk."

"What about your uncle?"

"What about my uncle?"

"Didn't you say he had a restaurant? He could feed Major the leftovers from people's plates and let him sleep out of the way somewheres. It would be no bother for him to take care of an old dog at a restaurant."

"My uncle is already letting me sleep in a

storeroom, and feeding me sometimes. I can't ask him to do me any more favors. How about your family if you're so big on saving him?"

"Didn't you say you wanted to work in your uncle's restaurant?" she asked, evading his question.

"Yeah, I do, but my father forbid him to hire me. If my father knew my uncle was giving me a room, he'd probably never speak to him again. See, my uncle is my father's youngest brother, and my uncle and I have always gotten along. He's kind of easygoing. Anyways, it makes my father mad. But when I'm legally of age, I can go to work for my uncle and maybe be partners with him someday."

"Your uncle would take Major if you asked him."

"I don't want to ask him. If I save Major today, I've still got to put down some other poor dog tomorrow. At least Major's lived a pretty good life."

She looked at the dog, who wagged not only his tail but his whole hind end at her attention. What could she do for him? Nothing. She bent and hugged him and let him slobber all over her cheek. When she looked up at Bill through tear-blurred eyes, she admitted, "I told someone you were my boyfriend."

"You did? Why'd you do that?"

"Because she has a boyfriend, and I wanted one, too. Are you mad that I lied about you?"

"You lie too much. You know that? You're going to get in trouble with all that lying."

"But you're not mad at me?"

"Just so long as you don't expect me to act like it's true."

"Don't you like me enough to be your girlfriend?"

"Betsy, you're a little kid. I like you, but you're only—you're too young for me to be your boyfriend."

"Three years is not such a big deal."

"Yeah, if you were twenty and I was twenty-three it wouldn't be. I'll tell you what. We'll wait till then and see how we feel about each other. O.K.?"

"You're treating me just the way my family does. I hate being laughed at."

"Oh, boy!" he said. "How'd I ever get myself into this? Will you get on home now? I've gotta get this job over with."

"Is Zoro doing all right?"

"He's fine."

"You wouldn't do anything about him without telling me, would you?"

"I said I wouldn't, and unlike some people, I don't lie."

"I'll write my phone number down. Then you could call me if you had to. Do you have a pencil?" She took the pencil he offered her and wrote her number neatly on the wall near the door to the gas chamber.

"Betsy!" he said in mild shock at her choice of a writing surface. "You're a terrible kid."

"Can I watch?" she asked soberly.

"What for?"

"Because I want to."

"I don't see what for. You'll get upset."

"I don't want to just walk away and let it happen."

"Anyway, it's not as bad as you think," he said. "It goes fast." Abruptly he opened the metal door, lifted Major and set him down inside. Major looked up and whimpered. Bill shut the door firmly and went into the compartment next to the box of a room. He turned on some valves. "It'll be over in a few minutes. He won't feel a thing. He just goes to sleep. I leave the light on so he won't be too scared."

She shuddered and was silent.

He looked at her with concern. "The other way to do it is by injection. Mr. Berrier does that. He injects something into their heart that kills them instantly. It doesn't hurt. They don't know what hit them."

"Yes, they do," she said. She stood beside him when he opened the door to the gas chamber. The dog lay on his side, dead.

"It's just like in the concentration camps they had in Germany," she said.

"No," Bill said. "Those were people."

"What's the difference? Animals are human, too."

"No, they're not."

"They are. They feel things. They know. They have a right to live, just as much right as people do."

"The thing is, a dog's dependent on someone to take care of him, and if there's no people to take care of him, he's gonna suffer. You don't want to see miserable, sick animals running around dying in the streets, do you?"

"I want to see them taken care of some place. We spend piles of money on bombs and stupid highways. Why couldn't we set up farms for animals nobody wants? Why couldn't we have foster homes for animals like we do for kids?"

"I don't know. Probably because nobody thinks animals are important enough."

"It's horrible," she said. "People are horrible."

Mr. Berrier appeared in the hall. "Bill," he said. "I thought you were going to come help me with that German shepherd."

"I'm coming right now, Mr. Berrier."

"You here again, Betsy? What are you doing, moving in on us?" Mr. Berrier joked.

"You—you *Nazi!*" she cried, and turned and hobbled out of the shelter, feeling a pain in her ankle that matched the pain in her heart. Outside, she pulled off her heels and walked home barefoot over the cold ground. When she could think again, she remembered that she hadn't asked Bill to help her solve the problem of getting Zoro out of the shelter and into the barn without arousing

Mr. Berrier's suspicions. What she had done instead was insult Mr. Berrier so that he would probably chase her away next time he saw her. A great morning—one enemy and plenty of material for a nightmare.

Chapter Eight

She kept seeing Major going to his death, his tail wagging amiably. The image blocked any other thought. Just because he was old. Just because people were so rotten. But Bill was nice even though he had been the executioner, and she loved animals but had stood there watching it. It didn't make any sense. She couldn't understand the contradictions. She didn't even have an idea of what she could have or should have done. She had never felt so helpless.

Saturday evening she drifted into the living room, hoping to find her father in a mood to talk. Sometimes he could explain things in a way that made them bearable. Once when she got scared because everybody at school believed in God and she couldn't seem to, he had said, "Then you're struggling to believe? If you're struggling, that's good. That's sure to be better in the eyes of any supreme deity than blind acceptance. Keep at it, Betsy. Struggle is what life's all about."

She found her father and Hal in the middle of another argument. Hal had been challenging Pops as long as Betsy could remember, but lately Hal sounded so contemptuous. Betsy didn't see why Pops let him get away with it.

"You mean they offered you a job and you turned it down?" Hal was highlighting every word with disbelief.

"I am at a stage of life where I don't have time to waste on dead-end jobs. Or don't you think your father has any right to look for fulfillment in his work, Hal?"

"You've always talked about the age of responsibility, Dad—when a guy stops being a kid. Haven't you reached the age of responsibility yet?"

"I don't see the need to justify myself to you, Hal. I have shouldered my responsibilities adequately all my married life. A breathing space, a hiatus, is not unreasonable now, and furthermore, it has nothing to do with you."

"Yes, it does. I don't even know if I should bother applying to private colleges next fall or if I'm stuck having to start out in a community college. Money makes plenty of difference."

"If you're smart enough, you can get a scholarship."

"Sure, Dad, every day—a full scholarship to Harvard, right? I'm sure they're just waiting for little old B-plus-average, nose-to-the-grindstone Hal."

"You want everything handed to you?"

"Not everything, just what's right. Didn't your parents send you to the college you wanted?"

"My father was a businessman. He wanted to be a businessman. It was easy money for him. Times are different now. Even if I were still teaching. You know, a guarantee of a college education doesn't come with your birth certificate."

"Mom promised me."

"Then what are you bugging me about? Go ask your mother. She'll no doubt stand ready to go into hock for her favorite son."

"Her only son."

"Ah, I knew there had to be some excuse for her foolishness." Pops grinned as if he had won something, but his eyes were hurt. Betsy advanced, touched his arm, and when he drew her close to him, she settled onto his bony lap.

"What do you think, Betsy? Shouldn't your old father have a chance to strike off in a new direction?"

"Whatever you do is right, Popsy."

"There's my little girl."

"Screw it!" Hal said. "I'll figure out a way to

make some big money on my own."

"What do you mean by that, Hal?" Mother asked, coming in with a full grocery bag in either arm.

"Nothing, Mom."

"What do you need big money for?" she persisted, frowning.

"Our foresighted son is worried about who's going to pay for his college education. He's implied that, because of an irresponsible and grossly self-centered father, his chances in life are blasted."

"Hal," Mother said. "Don't worry about the money for college. You get in where you want to go, and we'll figure out a way to pay for it together."

"Let me take those, Mom," he said, and relieved her of the bulging bundles.

"Amazing," Pops said, "how easy he is to get along with if you let him have his way all the time."

"He must get his pig-headedness from someone around here," Mother said dryly.

"I'll take the damn job, then!" Pops said and threw his glass across the room.

Betsy screamed and jumped out of his lap. Her mother turned and stalked down the hall to her bedroom. Mother never walked out on a fight. Betsy looked at Pops for an explanation.

He took a deep breath and said in a shaky voice, "Well, Betsy, that leaves you and me to clean up the mess. What do you say? Shall we sweep up the broken glass or let someone step in it?"

"Sweep it up," she said tonelessly and went for the dustpan and brush. Hal was in the kitchen, writing something furiously on a pad while he hugged the phone between his shoulder and his ear.

"Let me speak to Rick," Hal said into the receiver. "Then can you have him call me? I'll give you my number."

The house became very quiet after that. Hal took to his room.

When Betsy saw her father ready to turn on his stereo, she said to him, "Pops, I saw something awful at the animal shelter today."

"Betsy, not now, please. I've had enough emotional upheaval for one evening. I need a good dose of Bach to calm me down."

She drag-tailed down the hall to her own bedroom and thought of calling Karen, but it was Saturday night. Karen would be out with her boyfriend. Then she got out her daisy-bordered stationery to write to Phoebe, but she wasn't in the mood. Finally she wandered back through the living room to the dining area which they were using as a den. Her mother was there with the television on so low that it was barely audible.

"Mother?" When she didn't get an answer, Betsy walked around the Danish lounger to look at her mother's face and saw the tears. "What's wrong, Mother?"

"Nothing, Betsy. Sometimes everything begins to get to me, that's all."

"It does?" Betsy was amazed.

Once her mother told the family that she had been asked to describe herself in one word during a job interview. "What would you all have said about me?" Mother asked.

"Sensational," Pops had offered.

"Superwoman," Hal had said.

"That's two words," Betsy had said. "How about capable?"

"That's the word *I* used," Mother had said, smiling at Betsy.

"Can I help you?" she asked her mother now.

"No, thanks, honey. I'm just overreacting because I'm tired." She offered her hand in a gesture of welcome. Betsy took it and curled up on the couch beside her. She was tempted to offer her mother companionship in misery by telling her about Major, but then she remembered that her mother had forbidden her to go near the shelter at all. Better keep her mouth shut and concentrate on the movie on the television screen.

As she was falling asleep that night, Betsy saw the empty gas chamber in her mind. It woke her up, but suddenly the idea came to her. That was the way to get Zoro out, the perfect way. Tomorrow was Sunday and Bill would be off. She didn't know how to reach him by phone. She considered calling all the Chinese restaurants in town, but decided it would be wiser to wait until Monday. It would be all right. All she'd have to do was get Bill to tell a little white lie. Surely he wasn't going to object to that.

Chapter Nine

She hadn't been able to concentrate in school all day. A sixth sense that something was wrong kept nipping at her. Instead of going home first, she went directly from the school bus to the shelter. Bill was scrubbing out aluminum feeding bowls.

"Is Zoro all right?" she asked him anxiously.

He looked over his shoulder at her, then turned around and looked her up and down. "You look cute today, Betsy."

Cute! It figured. Just when she hadn't tried to impress him, he would notice how she looked. She glanced down at herself, having forgotten what she was wearing. A denim skirt, pale blue blouse and flat sandals—not even sexy since she'd forgotten the padded bra.

"Oh, you!" she said in disgust. "You don't know anything. How's Zoro?"

"Boy," he teased. "What kind of girlfriend would you make? All you care about is that dog."

"*My* dog. You're just keeping him for me, remember?"

"He's still the same. You come to visit him or me?"

"You first."

"Well, whichever—you better not let Mr. Berrier see you."

"He won't chase me."

"You called him a Nazi, remember? Hurt his feelings so he'll probably never forget it. He asked me to discourage you from coming around, said you're a nuisance."

"I'll go apologize to him."

"He's off on a call. Some kid got bit by a stray dog."

"Really? What happens to the dog, then?"

"First they have to make sure the dog doesn't have rabies. Otherwise the kid has to get shots and they're painful. Then, I don't know. It depends. Maybe nothing will happen."

She sat down on an upturned box. "I got it figured out—how to save Zoro without Mr. Berrier knowing."

"Yeah?" He stacked the last bowl and began rinsing out the sink.

"All we have to do is wait until Zoro's time is up. Then when you go to put him down, I whisk him out the back door and to the barn instead, and you tell Mr. Berrier Zoro's gone."

"Gone where?"

"Nowhere—just gone. Let him figure it out. He'll think Zoro's dead, probably, but you won't have been lying when you said he was gone."

"Pretty neat," he said after thinking it over for a moment. "Of course, it has a few holes in it."

"Where?"

"Suppose Mr. Berrier thinks I need help doing it? Or suppose he wants to see the body before we cremate it? Or he happens to hang around a lot that day. . . ."

"You can think of some way to get rid of Mr. Berrier."

"Me? How come I'm into this thing, anyway? Do you realize if I got caught, it would mean my job? Mr. Berrier's a nice guy, but if you're not straight with him, he gets mad. And he's already mad at you."

"You won't lose your job."

"Who's going to guarantee that? You?"

"It just won't happen. He wouldn't fire you just for helping me."

"I wouldn't be too sure of that."

"But Bill, you have to help me. I don't have anybody else."

"Yeah, but I don't know if I can get a job anyplace else, either."

"Please, please, please! I need you, please!" she begged.

"So that's why you like me," he said. "Because you need me to help you save Zoro." He might have been teasing. She couldn't tell.

"That's not true! I like you a lot because—just because."

"If you had to choose between Zoro and me, who'd you pick?" The smile showed in his eyes.

She looked at him in distress. Who would she pick? Zoro, of course. "Zoro hasn't got anybody but me," she said. Then all at once she couldn't stand there pleading with him any more. She turned her back on him and fled home.

The following Saturday her mother called her to the phone. "You said I should call you," Bill's voice said. "So I'm calling, but there's nothing you can do. The boss is going to put Zoro down right now himself."

"How come?"

"Something happened. I haven't got time to tell you now. Mr. Berrier's mad."

"Zoro did something. Tell me."

"Yeah . . . O.K. Listen fast. This guy comes and says he's been robbed twice and he lives alone and wants a dog in the house just for protection. He says he knows dogs and can handle anything. So Mr. Berrier warned him about Zoro, but the guy likes Zoro's looks and says we should just go away and he'll make friends with him. So time goes by and all of a sudden we hear this terrific commotion. When we run in, there's Zoro going right for the guy's throat. We had to beat the dog off the guy to make him let go."

"Did Zoro get hurt?"

"Oh, Betsy, what kind of question is that? It doesn't matter, anyway. Mr. Berrier is going to tie him up and give him a needle as soon as he gets done with some lady out there. This place has been a madhouse today."

"I'll be right over," she said and hung up.

She flew across the yard barefoot, barely touching the ground, without any idea of what she would do when she got there.

Mr. Berrier was busy concluding an adoption when she walked in. She was panting so loudly the family who were adopting the two five-month-old brother and sister beagle pups turned to stare at her. She ignored them and sat down to wait.

Mr. Berrier glared at her but didn't say anything while the people were standing there. The pups were shivering in the hands of a pair of boys who looked about five or six years old. The pups had never eaten or moved inside or out except together, and Betsy was glad they were being adopted together, though she thought six-year-old boys might be too rough for such timid animals. Mr. Berrier looked very pleased, though. He loaded the boys' parents up with pamphlets and advice and showed them how best to hold the quaking pups.

"Now, they haven't had any shots except distemper. We give all our new admittances distemper shots, but you ought to take them to a vet and have them checked over for worms and . . ."

Betsy slipped into the corridor and found Bill. "When Mr. Berrier's done, will you bring him down to Zoro's cage, please?"

"Why? What are you going to do?"

"You'll see."

"Things were going so good," Bill moaned. "We got four dogs adopted just this morning."

"Mr. Berrier's not going to put Zoro down. You'll see," Betsy said grimly.

She glanced at the identifying card in the pocket stuck to the front of Zoro's cage and stopped to read it. "Purebred Doberman, male, two years old, rabies inoculation, watchdog," and—there for all the world to see—"This dog bites."

Zoro was lying with his head on his paws facing the back wall as if he wanted to be alone. He lifted his head and looked at her through glazed eyes when he heard her unlatching the door of his cage. Then he got to his feet, teetering as if they had beaten him so hard he was still groggy.

"Zoro," she said softly. "Zoro, it's me."

At first his ears went back and he slunk into a corner as if she were an enemy, but she kept talking to him and crouched, calling him. Slowly he seemed to understand who it was, but instead of coming to her, he drooped and went back to the position she had first seen him in. If she had ever seen a picture of despair, he was it. She crept close to him. Her touch was light as a butterfly on his head. He didn't move. "Zoro, I'm here," she said. "You're not alone."

He sighed and lifted his head and lay on his side, his stump of a tail giving one feeble wag. "I'm not going to leave you now," she said. "They can make a card for me if they want. 'Betsy, thirteen-year-old female, all shots. Characteristics: funny-looking and dumb!'" Probably nobody would want to adopt her, either.

"They just don't understand you. You're really so beautiful," she said to Zoro, who accepted her cheek against his neck and seemed to ask in his soft whine what was worrying her. "You're in such big trouble," she said. "Such big trouble, and it isn't fair. You don't mean to be bad. You don't—" Both she and Zoro looked up at the sound of footsteps coming down the corridor toward them.

"You again!" Mr. Berrier exploded. "Now what are you trying to do, commit suicide?" His face had turned the color of chewed gum.

"Mr. Berrier, I'm really sorry I called you a Nazi. I know you're a nice man and you don't want to kill innocent animals."

"Get out of that cage this minute," Mr. Berrier roared as if he hadn't even heard her apology.

"I just want you to see that Zoro is a good dog. Look." She put her arms around the dog's body, her cheek against his jaw. Zoro, who had struggled to his feet at the approach of Bill and Mr. Berrier, ignored her. He was intent on Mr. Berrier.

"You're crazy. You are the craziest kid I've ever met, bar none."

"But you can see how he likes me. You can see that he's a good dog, can't you?"

"Yeah, I can see he's a good dog for you, but you're the only one in this world that dog's any good for, and you're not enough. Now come out of there."

"Not until you promise me you won't kill him."

"You threatening me? Listen kid, if there's one thing I don't put up with it's blackmail. I'm a patient man, but that's where my patience ends. Bill, go get the catchpole."

"What's a catchpole?" Betsy asked, worried.

"It's to handle dangerous animals at a distance. Now you listen to me while we're waiting here. I'm no Nazi. Bill can tell you the number of times I've given an animal extra time just because. Like last week we had a hound would charge the gate every time a customer came by, but let him out and he was docile as a baby. Well, his time come, and he come up and laid his paw on my arm like he was asking me. So instead of putting him down that day, I put him back in his cage, and you know what? The next day that dog was adopted."

"Good," Betsy said, standing up with her hand on Zoro's back. "That's a nice story."

"Well, it's true. Although he wandered off and

got lost right after they adopted him, the stupid mutt."

She said nothing. Bill came back with the catchpole. It had a leather noose at one end which could tighten up to hold an animal as small as a mouse. "O.K., now," Mr. Berrier said, "when I open that cage, you'll see what a sweetheart your dog is. With you in there, he's sure to attack because he's going to think he's protecting you."

Before Betsy understood how the pole worked, Mr. Berrier had deftly lassoed Zoro's head and was tugging him toward the gate which Bill had opened.

"No," Betsy screamed. "No!"

Her scream sent Zoro into a frenzy. He leaped and twisted, contorting his body to get loose and fighting so violently that he pulled the pole out of Mr. Berrier's hands. But when the dog then tried to jump out of the cage with the noose still around his neck, the pole slammed up crosswise against the opening, pulling Zoro up short. He yelped in pain. Betsy threw herself at him and tugged at the choking noose. No sooner did she free him than he jumped to his feet and launched himself at Mr. Berrier. Bill stepped in front of Mr. Berrier and knocked Zoro sideways.

"Zoro! Stop. Sit. Sit," Betsy screamed. She ran to the opposite end of the corridor and called him over and over by name. He hesitated, quivering and growling at Mr. Berrier and Bill, but his ears were half cocked toward Betsy. Finally, he turned away from the men and trotted to her, turning around so that he stood in a position to defend Betsy with his head facing back toward his enemies.

"All right. All right," Mr. Berrier said. "You win. I'll keep him around another few days, though what for I can't imagine. He's a menace. He's going to kill somebody yet. But all right. You get him back in the cage. Get him back in and, Lord knows, maybe a miracle will save him after all."

"If I was a dog, I'd sure want you on my side," Bill said when Zoro was back in his cage resting. Mr. Berrier had returned to the office and everything was back to normal.

"Why?" she asked suspiciously.

"The way you fought for him. That was really something."

"I care about people, too," she said defensively.

"Not as much as animals, I'll bet."

"That's not true!" she protested, but plodding home, she wasn't so sure. Who would she fight for the way she had fought for Zoro? Bill, if he needed her, maybe. But he could fight perfectly well for himself. Her father, but her mother was always taking care of him, putting him first, even before Hal. Would she fight for Hal if he needed her? Betsy thought about Hal's angry outburst that miserable evening when everyone had been unhappy. Since that night, Hal had been keeping to himself as if he weren't part of the family any more. He was so independent. She couldn't imagine he would ever need her. But he was her brother, and there had been times when he'd been nice to her. Yes, she'd fight for Hal.

Only when she was in the kitchen and saw her mother cleaning the oven did it occur to Betsy that she hadn't considered Mother in her list of people who mattered enough for her to defend. But she loved her mother. Of course she did. It was just that her mother, of all the people she knew, least needed anybody's help.

Chapter Ten

When Bill told her about Mr. Berrier's phone call to the sister of the old lady who had owned Zoro, Betsy didn't understand. "What did he do that for?"

"He wanted to find out how come Zoro lets you near him and nobody else. He said there had to be a reason.

"Is there a reason?"

"Yeah. It seems the old lady took Zoro because she knew he only attacked males. See, it was a man and his sons who tried to make a guard dog out of him when he was a puppy by beating and starving him, but there was a woman living with them who was kind to Zoro, so that's why he's O.K. with females. Then along comes the old lady who figures anybody breaking into her store was gonna be male. She didn't have any male relatives—it was just her and her sister. So she kept Zoro chained during the day when customers came in and let him run loose in the store at night."

After the long story, all Betsy said was, "Oh."

"Are you disappointed?"

"About what?"

"That it's just because you're female that he likes you?"

"No, I'm glad. That means he's only half as mean as Mr. Berrier thinks, and all I have to do is get him to trust men."

"Yeah, right, nothing to it. But you know what? Until you retrain him, we better stall on transferring Zoro to the barn. If some little guy ever got in the barn by accident, you know what would happen."

"I could put a lock on the door."

"Yeah, but till you tame Zoro, it's risky—if you can tame Zoro."

She saw his point. Her nighttime sessions with Zoro became training hours. She and Bill rigged up a straw dummy which hung from a long rope. They managed to loop it over a beam so that Betsy could jig the dummy to simulate movement and teach Zoro not to attack it. Again at Bill's suggestion, she dressed the dummy with items of clothing from various members of her family, from Bill and even from Mr. Berrier. She would sneak out a jacket or a pair of pants, use it for a training

session and next day return it to the hamper or
the closet or the back of a chair on which she had
found it. Zoro responded well when she stood
right beside him telling him, "No. Stay." But if
she made him stay and left his side to operate the
dummy from another point in the barn away from
him, he would whine and fidget about, yearning
to come to her. Then if the dummy happened to
swing in his direction, he would lose control and
attack. Still, Betsy felt certain she was making
progress with him. At least Zoro no longer
growled at Bill, nor tried to attack him, though he
cowered when Bill touched him.

Betsy decided that the next day when Bill was
on duty and Mr. Berrier was off would be it. The
only thing left was to make up some excuse to explain why Bill had put Zoro down without Mr.
Berrier's instructions.

April slipped into May without anything
special enough happening to put a label on the
days. Karen volunteered to work on the food com-
mittee for the big eighth-grade party, so Betsy
volunteered, too. Her mother picked her up at
school after the late Wednesday afternoon meet-
ings. Sometimes Betsy had a whole hour alone
with Karen to talk while they waited to be driven
home.

The second week Betsy confessed, "I lie a lot,
Karen, to make myself sound big."

"You do? Why do you want to do that?" Karen
asked.

"I don't know. Usually I guess it's because I don't have something I'd like to have, so I pretend. Like I told you Bill was my boyfriend. He's not really my boyfriend, not like Ken is for you. Do you think I'm awful?"

"What else did you lie about?" Karen asked cautiously, her fair, friendly face clouded by a frown.

"Nothing that I can think of now—to you. I lied a lot to Bill when I first met him, but he caught on to me pretty quick."

"What did you lie about to him—or is that private?"

"You're my best friend. Nothing's too private to share with you. We can talk to each other about anything, can't we?"

"Well, almost anything."

"What don't you tell me?" Betsy wanted to know, jealous of Karen's secrets.

"Oh, you know, sometimes things about my parents. I don't think it's nice to talk about your parents even to your closest friends."

"Oh, I agree," Betsy said quickly though she had never thought about that before.

"So what did you lie to Bill about?" Karen asked again.

"Dumb things, like my age—but he knows now. And then about a dog at the shelter. I told him my parents were going to let me adopt Zoro, but they weren't really."

"Who's Zoro?"

Betsy started describing Zoro. She talked about how intelligent he was and how badly he had been treated and how she wanted to save him. She talked about the shelter itself, too, and what went on there.

Karen's eyes grew wide with dismay and she said, "I think it's terrible that they kill all those animals, just awful. I'll never take any animal there now—never."

"But if you found a stray and you couldn't keep it, what would you do with it?"

"Put an ad in the paper. Keep him until somebody took him."

"But if nobody did?"

"I don't know, Betsy." Karen looked stricken.

"I don't know, either." Betsy wished someone sometime would offer a solution.

"Anyway, you won't tell me any more fibs, will you?" Karen asked.

The old-fashioned word "fibs" amused Betsy. Sometimes Karen sounded like a Sunday school text. But she was a generous, loyal friend. Betsy felt lucky that Karen liked her. "No," Betsy said. "I won't lie to you ever again."

Had Karen not put family off limits for discussion, Betsy would have confided in her about how her family was falling apart. It disturbed Betsy. Sometimes she felt as if they had all left her behind, alone in the space where the heart of their family used to be. She didn't like being left. She didn't like being alone, either.

Even her mother, who used to be there for any-one who needed her, seemed preoccupied lately. She had handed over the field-trip money Betsy had asked her for, but the next day she acted as if Betsy hadn't explained what the money was to be used for, though Betsy knew she had gone into great detail about the bus and the picnic lunch and the museum they were to see. It wasn't Pops Mother seemed worried about, either, but Hal.

Betsy noticed that Mother had begun to nag Hal about where he spent his free time. She had never done that before. Hal always had had more freedom to do what he wanted than any of them. "He can take care of himself. He's got the world by the tail," Mother always said. But now she kept asking him about his new friends, and why he had come in so late the night before. There was someone called Rick about whom Mother kept questioning Hal. He wasn't giving her straight answers, though. He wasn't taking Mother's side any more, either, when Pops and Betsy neglected a household chore. In fact, Hal seemed to avoid them all. Mostly, he wasn't home.

One evening when Betsy walked into the kitchen for a snack, Mother was saying, ". . . because I found your bankbook, Hal, and I don't understand where all that money went."

"You looked inside my bankbook? That's rotten, Mom. A bankbook is private."

"Is it? Then why did you leave it on your dresser? You left your room in a mess for me to clean up instead of doing it yourself. If I found something I wasn't supposed to find, whose fault is it?"

"I was in a hurry," he said sullenly.

"I think you'd better talk to me about it, Hal."

"There's nothing to talk about."

Betsy took a pear from the fruit bowl and went to the sink to wash it. Her mother and brother looked at her as if she weren't there, but they did stop talking. What was going on? She wondered if they'd ever stop treating her like a baby and begin confiding in her.

Then Pops decided that he was never going back to the teaching he had hated so much. Instead, he'd become a writer. Suddenly the atmosphere in the house improved. He took to his typewriter with enthusiasm. All over the house Betsy could hear the irregular tapping of the keys. Whatever he was writing put him in a better mood. He didn't always have a cigarette in his hand now and he wasn't always complaining. She hoped what he was writing would make him rich and famous.

He had begun to tease her again now that he was feeling happier. "I think you've reached that age, Betsy."

"What age, Pops?"

"The blossoming age. I see distinct signs of bloom on you. You're looking pretty cute. Unless it's more than just maturation. You don't have a boyfriend, do you?"

"Almost."

"An almost boyfriend? Well, is he as handsome as your father?"

"I don't know. I just like him."

"So soon, huh? I thought you were going to be my girl for years yet."

"You're still my favorite, Popsy. You don't have to worry about losing me."

"There's my baby!" He gave her a quick hug which she returned happily. Nobody was more fun than her father when he was in a good mood. He hadn't been in a really good mood for so long she had forgotten how lovable he could be.

At the shelter that afternoon while she was drinking a Coke with Bill, Betsy thought of what her father had said about her blooming. She glanced sideways at Bill. "You wouldn't want to take me to a movie or something like that sometime, would you?" she tested.

He got that sparkle in his eye that meant he thought she was funny. "I might want to, but I can't afford to."

"If I paid, could we go sometime?"

"If you paid? Well, maybe. I've got to save as much of my salary as I can."

"What for?"

"So I can go back to school eventually and graduate and maybe even go to college."

"I thought you quit because you hated school."

"No, I don't really hate it. Some parts of it I miss, like friends and fooling around with other kids. I just hated my father pushing me all the time. I don't know, I may end up going to work for my uncle instead of going to college, but in any case, I want to finish high school, and one thing I know for sure is I want to be independent."

"Your father must be really mean."

"No. He's just old-fashioned. He doesn't understand. No, I have a lot of respect for him. It's just I can't live with him on my back all the time."

"My brother is getting like that, I think. He used to be close to my mother, at least, but now it's like he's trying to break away from the family."

"Are you close to him?"

"My brother? No. He doesn't have any time for me. You make a better brother than he does."

"Oh, ho! This is a new one. Well, which is it—do you want me to be your brother or your boyfriend?"

She didn't have to think to answer, "Boyfriend."

"Betsy," he said, and his tone was serious now. "We better talk about this. I mean, you're a nice kid, but you can't really be my girlfriend. I mean, you're way too young. It's O.K. if you want to pretend. I mean, if it makes you feel good, I don't mind, but really, if I go back to school in the fall and you're going into high school then, too—well, you've just got to understand, you can't go around telling everybody you're my girlfriend."

She stared at him, then looked away.

"I'm sorry, Betsy. I don't want to hurt your feelings, but I don't want you to have the wrong idea, either. Are you mad at me?"

"I knew we were just pretending," she said shortly. She had known, but behind the knowing was the hope that maybe something could develop, that maybe pretend could become real. Why couldn't he be her boyfriend, after all?

"We're still friends, anyway, right?" he asked.

She nodded coolly, but she went home as soon after that as she could leave without appearing to be running away from him. She went immediately to her mother's dresser and stared at herself in the mirror, trying to see any signs of blooming her father had seen. She looked like a skinny, elfin-faced little girl in the mirror. It had been dumb to think even for a minute that Bill could be serious about having her be his girlfriend. Zoro was the only one who really liked her without any reservations.

Chapter Eleven

All that Friday it rained, sometimes soft and steady, sometimes in globules so heavy they bounced off the black macadam road and crested in miniature waves. Betsy had endured a double-period test in social studies and a vocabulary quiz that day. She came home with a headache, depressed by the weather and the certainty she had done badly. Never mind that she always expected to fail. This time she had for sure.

The phone was ringing when she dripped her way into the kitchen. She picked up the receiver with one wet hand while tugging off her sopping jacket with the other.

"It's all set up," Bill said, sounding as nervous as if he were talking about a crime they were going to commit.

"What did you tell Mr. Berrier?" Betsy asked.

"Well, see, the shelter's full right now, and he was saying that we'd have to start making some room again. Also he's going to this A.S.P.C.A. meeting in New York. So I figured this was as good a time as any, and I told him I'd pick one out and do it while he was gone. He was glad."

"Good. O.K. then, I'll come get Zoro. Or should we wait until it's dark to make sure nobody sees?"

"It's dark enough right now. Nobody's going to see anything in all this rain. Besides, you have to take him before I leave so I can say *I* did the job. Otherwise, if the guy who comes in tonight sees him in his cage, he's going to wonder what happened if you come in and take him out later." He was so nervous, his words tumbled over one another.

"All right, but you be sure there's nobody back there by the cages for the next ten or fifteen minutes. O.K.?"

"Betsy, I'm not good at lying. I hope I don't blow it when Mr. Berrier comes back and I tell him Zoro was the one I put down."

"You won't."

"I don't know. My father could take one look at me and know I was trying to get away with something."

"Don't worry," she said. "Mr. Berrier will swallow it easy. Just don't make too big of a story out of it."

"I have a feeling I'm going to end up without a job," he said gloomily.

To divert him, she teased, "I guess you must like me more than you think."

"Huh?"

"Well, you hate doing this, but you're doing it for me anyway."

"Yeah, I ought to have my head examined."

"It's nice you like me so much."

"Let's not exaggerate now."

She smiled into the receiver and fluttered her eyelashes. "Do you think I'm pretty, Bill?"

"Oh, come on, Betsy. Stop it now. This is serious."

She tossed her wet hair back. "Anyway, I know I'm not pretty. I just wanted to see what you'd say."

"O.K. I say good luck to both of us because if anything goes wrong and I lose my job, I don't know what I'm going to do."

"Don't worry. If you run out of money, I'll support you."

"Sure. I can move into the barn with Zoro and you'll feed us both."

"Right. I hope you find dog food tasty."

Transferring Zoro from his cage to the barn took five minutes. He seemed to think the rain was fun. He frisked about, inviting Betsy to play, looking up at her with his hind end in the air like a puppy. "This time you'll never have to go back to that cage," she promised him. She had pans ready in the barn for water and his food, and a pile of ripped-up newspapers in the far corner which he seemed to have chosen for his bathroom area. His bed was an old beach blanket on top of the burlap sacks. Betsy didn't have a lock for the door yet, and she didn't know how she was going to get Zoro from the barn to a permanent home in her backyard, but she expected, since they'd come this far, the rest of the rescue operation would work out, too.

By Saturday morning the rain had settled down to stay. Betsy slipped out early to pay Bill for the big bag of dog meal he had bought for her. He reported that Mr. Berrier had been so relieved to be rid of Zoro he hadn't asked any questions at all.

On her way home, she stopped at the barn, full of optimism, especially when she saw how contented Zoro seemed. He licked her face in greeting and squirmed all over with delight. Her mother had enlisted Betsy in too many errands for her to spend much time with Zoro during the day, but she told him she would be back in the evening.

She volunteered to do the dishes after dinner so that she could collect the table scraps for Zoro. Mother was pleasantly surprised at Betsy's offer.

"It's easy with just three of us," Betsy explained.

Hal had not shown up for dinner. Speculation on that occupied her parents all the while Betsy was lowering her plastic container of scraps and a jar full of water out her bedroom window. Then she walked back through the house so that she could leave by the front door empty-handed and not arouse their suspicions.

Even so, her mother asked, "Where are you going, Betsy?"

"Out for a walk."

"In this rain?"

"I like the rain."

"Since when? You used to hate it," Pops said.

"Well, I don't any more."

"Hal didn't say anything to you about where he was going tonight, did he?" Mother asked.

"Hal never says anything to me," Betsy said. "Stop worrying, Mother. He's probably just busy making money."

"Well, your father and I are going out tonight, and I don't like leaving you alone. That's why I wanted to know where Hal was."

"Don't worry about it. I'll be fine alone." She was in a hurry to get to Zoro and see how *he* was doing alone in the barn.

"I'll leave the number by the phone so you can reach us if you need us," Mother said. "Don't walk too far."

Two days of rain had turned the ground around the barn doors to mud. Zoro was so glad to see her that he barked. She shushed him and fed him. As soon as he finished eating, he came to her, and she wrapped her arms around him and hugged him. Then she let him see the tennis ball she had brought to play with. She tossed it up. His eyes followed it up and down, but he didn't move. Instead, he looked at her to see what she was going to do. "Like this, Zoro," she said and tried to show him how to run and catch the ball. Over and over again she threw the ball and ran around the familiar dusty areas of the barn after it. Zoro sat on his haunches and watched her, interested but with no notion of getting in the game.

"Didn't anybody ever play with you?" she asked him. She sat down beside him, weary from running in circles after the ball. He put his head on her lap and looked up at her adoringly. "I guess nobody ever did," she said and stroked the handsome narrow head. "If it stops raining soon, I'll take you out for a walk on a leash."

The barn was very dark. The only light came through the two small dirt-crusted windows facing the empty fields. The dust tickled Betsy's nose and the musty-smelling dampness was chilling. "It's not a very nice place," she said. "I hope I don't have to keep you locked in here too long." That reminded her. Where would she get a lock? She wondered if she could use the one they had made her buy for her gym locker. So what if anybody stole her sneakers and gym suit! Another thing she would have to do was figure out an excuse for hanging around the barn so much in case her family noticed. She could tell them she was building something in it for school, but they would want to know what. Maybe she *should* build something here—a doghouse for Zoro, an insulated one he could sleep in outdoors all winter. Maybe she could get Hal to help her. Except he was so busy these days. Besides, he'd probably tell their parents about Zoro the minute he saw them. Nothing further came to her in the way of ideas.

She began putting Zoro through his obedience lessons, keeping the commands simple and consistent the way Bill had told her to do it, making Zoro sit and stay and come. Zoro responded well. "Good boy," she told him. "Oh, you're such a good, good dog." She knew he could be trained to like people eventually. It was just a matter of being patient with him, and she had lots of patience, lots of time, too.

Without a watch, she didn't know how long she had been in the barn before the rain stopped. The scabby gray clouds peeled away to reveal a sapphire-blue evening sky with one star low on the horizon. Betsy took Zoro for a walk through the muddy fields, letting him investigate all the smells his inquisitive nose discovered while she concentrated on avoiding water-filled ruts. Zoro scared up a rabbit and chased it a ways until she called him back to her side. He walked, head up, looking as if joy tingled in every muscle of his sleek body. When he nudged her hand, she laid it on his head and so they walked circling the field. Her mind was empty of everything but the phosphorescent evening marked by forktailed swallows swooping overhead and the lulling chirp of the hidden insects.

The barn seemed darker than ever when they returned to it. The door creaked eerily as she pulled it shut behind them. Moonlight shafted across the floor. Betsy stared at it dreamily with her head resting against Zoro's flanks as he lay on his bed. She didn't want to stay too late. She had to be home when her parents returned. Still, she dozed for a few minutes.

The sound of a car stopping on gravel startled her awake. Someone at the animal shelter at this time of night? Who? Maybe the old man who slept there to keep watch had had to go out. She held her breath as she heard voices. Her heart drummed out fear and fear crept into her throat to choke her as the barn door swung open.

"How come it's not even closed? You sure this place is O.K.?" a strange boy's voice said.

"Sure it is. Nobody ever comes here. It's the safest place I can think of."

That was Hal. What was he doing in her barn? She clung to Zoro, whispering, "Stay, stay," into his ear. She could feel his muscles coiling. Hal wouldn't even give her a chance to explain if he found her here with the dog. She stroked Zoro's bony side, trying to calm him with slow, even motions. She could feel his heart beating too fast just as hers was. Go away, Hal, she begged in her head.

"Where are we going to hide the stuff?" the stranger asked.

"We can put it back there behind that pile of junk."

"I think we'd be safer burying it."

"God, Rick! You're so nervous, you're making me nervous," Hal said.

"If you'd done time like me, you'd be nervous, too. And don't kid yourself—what we've got here—if we get caught with it—we get sent up so we won't get out till our hair turns gray."

"Yeah, well—we're not going to get caught. Come on, Rick. How many do you suppose they catch out of everybody in the country who deals a little? The odds are with us if you don't panic. All we have to do is keep the deliveries separate from the cash transactions and nobody's going to suspect."

"Yeah, yeah, I heard you. I know. Wouldn't of took you in if I didn't trust you. You're smart. I know. Last guy I worked with wasn't so smart—or maybe he was. I was the one got caught."

Betsy tried to peer around the post that marked off the loft from the floor of the barn. Even so slight a movement caught the attention of the boy Hal had called Rick.

"What's that? I hear something."

"Mice, probably. That's why I suggested this old garbage can. We don't want the rodents getting high on all this pot."

"Yeah, O.K. So let's start making up the orders. You got the light?"

A cone of ghostly light joined the moon's radiance and Rick jumped.

"That's too bright. Somebody will see lights in the barn and come to see what's going on."

"Rick, relax. There's no windows on the sides that face the buildings. Nobody's going to see the light. You got the list?" Hal sounded bored with his companion's nervousness. Betsy settled into a more comfortable position for waiting. It was beginning to dawn on her that Hal was doing something bad, something that might get him into trouble.

Suddenly Zoro sneezed. "Somebody's there!" Rick cried. "Let's get out of here."

"Hold it. I'll go see. Give me that flashlight," Hal said. Before she could think of what to do, the flashlight was shining in Betsy's eyes.

"What the hell are you doing here?" Hal yelled.

With her eyes squeezed shut against the light, Betsy tried hard to hold on to Zoro, but the dog surged out of her arms, aimed like a breaking wave at Hal's throat. Hal went down with the dog on top of him. Betsy did a flat dive after Zoro and grabbed him around his middle, but she couldn't pry him loose from Hal, who was screaming in terror.

"Stop! Stop, Zoro! No, no, no!" she wailed at the snarling dog. With all her strength she rammed her shoulder into Zoro's belly, but she couldn't budge him, and the cruel teeth were mauling Hal's upraised arm.

"Watch out," Rick said. Betsy looked up in time to see the two-by-four descending. She ducked. Zoro yelped and dropped to the ground, letting go of Hal, who rolled out of the way, scrambled to his feet and staggered over to the barn door. There he faltered, but Rick shoved the door open for him.

"You all right, Hal?" Rick asked.

"My arm—he slaughtered me," Hal sobbed.

In the light from the flashlight which Rick shone on Hal, Betsy saw the blood streaming from her brother's torn upper arm. She gasped, too full of anguish to breathe. Then she bent her head to Zoro, who was lying still where Rick had struck him down.

"Who are you?" Rick asked her.

"I'm Betsy, Hal's sister."

"I got to get Hal to the emergency room," Rick said. She looked up. He was talking to her. "I'll take him, but what are *you* going to do?"

"Stay here." She thought she could hear a heartbeat. If Zoro was dying, she wanted to be with him, to comfort and hold him.

"No, I mean about what you just heard. About what's in this pail."

"I'm not going to do anything."

"How do I know that?"

"Because I promise. Do you think I want to get

my brother in trouble? Hurry up before he bleeds to death, will you?"

Rick hesitated. Hal slumped against the doorpost saying, "I'm gonna pass out."

"Please hurry. Please take him to the hospital," she begged, frightened by the signs of Hal's weakness.

With a last suspicious glance flung at her like a warning, Rick went into action. He put his arm around Hal, letting him lean on him though Hal was taller and heavier than he. They struggled out the door.

Betsy waited, barely breathing, until she heard the sound of the car starting up and the gravel being kicked up by turning wheels. She looked around the now silent barn, unable to believe the disasters of the last few minutes. But the dented metal garbage can was there and Zoro was lying still on his side, a dark outline in the pool of moonlight. She took the flashlight that had been knocked aside in the commotion and sat down beside her dog to examine him closely. When she touched his shoulder, he whined in pain.

"But you're still alive," she whispered. Still alive, but not for long. They would put him down now without question. Tomorrow, as soon as Hal told her parents, as soon as anyone asked where the dog was who had mauled him. "Now you've done it," she said to him sorrowfully.

In the barn nothing stirred, nothing sounded but the chirr of insects outside and a creaking as the door swung on its hinges in the light wind. She stroked his head with the very tips of her fingers, crooning his name. She felt nothing, thought nothing, heavy with despair.

The sound of a car passing on the road startled her. Suppose the police came! She looked at the garbage can and thought of Hal in the emergency ward. His arm had looked so chewed up. She didn't want him crippled. "Don't let him be badly hurt," she prayed. "Let his arm be all right." Then she thought about what was in the garbage pail. He had never done anything dishonest before. Suppose he got caught? Jail would be worse than any injury. That fear in Rick's voice when he had talked about doing time!

Hal and the bank account Mother had questioned him about—that had something to do with it. Mother suspected he was doing something illegal. Probably he had withdrawn money to buy the pot. But Mother hadn't known how to stop him. And Hal was angry at Pops. He wanted to go to college so bad. He had always talked about college, where he would go, so serious, always planning for his future, and now he was in trouble. She wished she had someone she could talk to, someone who'd give her good advice. But who would she dare tell about what was in that dented metal pail hiding in the shadows of the barn? Her father? Her mother? She had promised Rick she wouldn't talk about it. Then what could she do?

Rabies shots, she thought suddenly. She had to tell the hospital that the dog that bit Hal had had his rabies shots. She dashed across the mucky yard for home and looked up the emergency room number in the telephone book. Once she had spoken to the admissions clerk there and promised to send Zoro's record card along as proof, she found herself with a solution for Hal's trouble in her mind.

She got a shovel from the garage, took it back to the barn and tested the ground around the barn door until she found the old manure pile where she could dig in deep easily. Not much time was left if she was going to finish before her parents got back from their party. It was already after ten according to the clock in their kitchen. She dug a shallow pocket in the mud and dragged the garbage pail outside. It seemed to be half full of plastic-wrapped cakes of what looked like peat moss in the dark. Hastily she tore away the plastic wrapping. Then she began breaking up the cakes with the shovel and digging the dried matter under. She worked it in so that it was too well mixed with mud to be sifted out. Cake by cake she continued until the garbage pail was empty and blisters rose on her palms. They hurt when she touched the shovel's handle. Her shoulders ached, too, and she was so tired that she wanted nothing more than to stumble home to bed, but she kept digging up more dirt and piling it on top of the buried marijuana. At last she could hardly lift her arms to do anything. She took the shovel into the barn with her.

Zoro lifted his head and whined at her. She went to him. Once the stub of his tail wagged for her, just once. Awkwardly he pushed with three legs until he was standing. His left front leg hung limp below the smashed shoulder.

"I could take you to a vet," she said, "but what good would that do? They'd fix your shoulder and kill you anyway, maybe just kill you first." She sat beside him in discouragement. He licked her cheek. "Good dog," she murmured. "My good dog." He was good. From his point of view, he'd been protecting her. How did he know Hal was her brother and not some stranger out to attack her?

An image appeared in her head of the empty appliance store with the For Sale sign that her school bus passed every morning. It wasn't far. She could hide Zoro there if she could get in. If she could get him that far, if he could walk on his own. She ran to the door, turned and called him to her. He lurched toward her on three legs and whimpered when his injured limb touched the floor. He'd never make it that way.

"Wait here, then. Stay," she said. She ran, too dazed to think more than one step ahead, but pushed into action by a terrible sense of urgency.

She found her father's wheelbarrow and a rope and rolled the barrow back to the barn. There she lined it with the burlap sacks and old beach blanket that had been Zoro's bed. Then she positioned the wheelbarrow vertically next to him and coaxed and pushed and hoisted him in. He yelped in agony once and once he snarled, but he didn't fight her as she half expected he might. It seemed as if he knew she was trying to help him, and he was cooperating as best he could.

When she finally had him lying in the wheelbarrow she tied the rope four ways around, packaging him in. Then, rising above her own weariness, she pushed the barrow out of the barn, across the back of the shelter's property and out to Blue Barns Road.

The store was only a quarter of a mile to the left, but she was so exhausted that she worried she might have to stop and give up before she got him there. Cars swished past, their headlights blinding her as their high beams raked over her. She trudged on in the cavernous darkness below the trees. Each time a car passed she held her breath, afraid it would stop and someone inquire what she was doing out alone at night pushing a wheelbarrow with a dog in it who kept craning his head to see where she was taking him, then looking up at her anxiously. The road stretched on and on, black tunnel below an ink-blue sky in a dream which would never release her. Only the pain in her hands and back and shoulders and legs was real, the pain and Zoro.

There it was! She saw the For Sale sign in the momentary glare of passing headlights. She

scrunched cautiously over the gravel parking area
around to the side, holding her breath in hopes
there would be some easy way in. There was a
side door, but it was locked. Now what? Had it
all been for nothing? How would she get food to
Zoro here, anyway? It wouldn't be any good. Use-
less to have lugged him all this way. She got up to
circle the building just to make sure. The moon il-
luminated the broken window in back for her.
Hope gave her new energy. Carefully she climbed
through the opening into a closet-sized bathroom.
From there she walked into the back room of the
store. Empty shelves, nothing else. Perfect!

She opened the side door from the inside. Zoro
had struggled loose from the ropes and was out of
the wheelbarrow, licking his wounded shoulder.
She encouraged him to hobble into the storeroom.
This had been the place he had been required to
guard, and he whined and headed for a corner
next to the shelf where he collapsed and began
licking his shoulder again.

"It's the best hiding place I can think of, Zoro,"
Betsy told him. "Nobody's going to think of looking for you here. You'll be O.K. for a while until I
can think what to do."

She set up his bed in a corner of the empty
room. He lay trembling, watching her. "Do you
hurt so much? But you're safe here and tomorrow
you'll feel better," she said and kissed him. She
settled him on his bed and petted him for a while.
Then she tried the water in the bathroom sink, re-

lieved to find it hadn't been turned off. A soap dish made an inadequate water bowl for Zoro, but he lapped it empty gratefully each of the four times she filled it for him. Tomorrow she could bring his food and water dishes and dog meal and then think what to do next.

She left the wheelbarrow, too tired to get anything else besides herself home. She cut through the shelter's property toward her house and was just passing the barn when the screech of brakes and the sound of a car door jerking open made her look back over her shoulder. Rick! She wanted to run away, but she could barely move. No place to hide, either. Rick strode over to her.

"O.K., I left him at the hospital. They'll take care of him."

"Is he all right?" Betsy asked, trying to hide her fear of Rick.

"He's a mess, but he'll live, if that's what you mean. That dog really tore him up good."

She started to edge away.

"Where are you going?" he asked.

"Home. I'm tired."

"I want to talk to you first."

"I'm not going to tell anybody anything. Not even my parents. You're safe." She didn't know what he might do to her if he found out what she had done with the marijuana, but she kept her voice steady and started walking past him. He grabbed her arm.

"I said I want to talk to you." His voice was tense.

"You hurt my dog."

"You better thank me. He would've killed your brother."

"No," she said. The tears started from her eyes.

"That dog's a killer."

"No."

"It doesn't matter, anyways. Now listen, I'm going to take that garbage can away—"

"It's empty."

"What?"

"I dumped all the stuff out and buried it."

His thin face hung open with surprise. "You hid it somewheres?"

"No. I buried it in the manure pile. Go see for yourself."

"Why'd you do that? That stuff is worth a fortune."

"I don't want my brother dealing."

"You're crazy!"

"Now you don't have to worry about going to jail again."

"You—" He raised his hand to hit her, but she yanked loose and fled toward home, spurred on by fear, not slowing down, not even aware that he wasn't following her. Her parents were just driving into the garage.

"Mom!" she screamed. "Mom! You've got to go to the hospital to see Hal. He came into the barn looking for me and my dog attacked him."

"What? What dog? What are you talking about, Betsy?"

"Just go to the hospital to the emergency ward. Rick brought him there."

"Rick? Oh, my God!"

She didn't dare stay home alone. They took her with them in the car to the hospital, and there they deserted her in the waiting room. Hours passed. She was too numb with exhaustion to be impatient. Finally, she stretched out on a plastic-covered couch and fell asleep, so sound asleep she didn't feel her father pick her up and carry her to the car and home to bed.

Chapter Twelve

Betsy woke up and wondered why she ached so. Was she sick? Then awareness jolted through her. What had she done? Hal was in the hospital. Zoro had attacked him. When she had space for another thought, she hoped Hal wasn't in pain. She hoped his arm would heal fast. She hoped he wasn't hating her. She would buy him a present and visit him in the hospital unless he refused to see her. He might hate her, if not because of Zoro, then because of what she had done with the contents of his garbage can. She'd have to tell him about it when he asked, or Rick would tell him. In any case, he'd know soon.

She got up and looked out the window. The yard was full to the brim with sunshine. Soft blue sky, lacy spring green on the trees. A beautiful day, but Zoro was waiting for her in the store, and she had a lot more lies to tell. She looked at her hands, blistered from last night's digging. What could she tell them had happened to Zoro? He had run away? Then they'd go looking for him, and if he barked and someone happened to be passing the empty store—poor dog. He must be in such pain, and hungry besides. Suppose his shoulder didn't heal by itself? She had to get food to him sometime today. Tomorrow she would have to go to school again. If Rick wanted to come after her, he could find her at school easily enough. He could lie in wait for her, beat her up with a stick the way he had beaten Zoro. She curled back under the covers to hide from the thought and from the morning and the night before. But no hiding place protected her from remembering.

"Betsy?" Pops called outside her room.

"Uhhh."

"Are you awake yet?"

"Almost."

He opened the door and sat down at the foot of her bed. "It's nearly noon," he said, looking at her critically. "And I think you have a lot to tell me."

"About Zoro?"

"Hal says you must have been keeping him in the barn."

"I was."

"Hal says the dog attacked with no provocation."

"He was trying to protect me. He's—he just doesn't like men, but he's not really a bad dog. He's—"

"Why were you keeping him in the barn?"

"They were going to put him down. I rescued him."

Pops took a deep breath. "We want to go back to the hospital to see Hal soon."

"How is Hal?"

"He'll need physical therapy after the arm heals."

"I feel so awful, Pops."

"Well, you have reason to feel awful. If you hadn't been idiot enough to try to save a vicious dog, your brother wouldn't be suffering the way he is. I hope you learned something from this experience."

"What?"

"You tell me. How do you feel about what you did?"

For a minute she was confused. Was he talking about Zoro or that she had buried the pot? But Hal wouldn't have told on himself—not likely. It had to be Zoro her father meant. "I'm sorry," she said.

"You should be," he said. "Well, that's something for starters. Next thing is, do you know where the dog is?"

"Zoro?"

"Betsy, no stalling. Unless you don't mean it when you say you're sorry."

She needed more time to think, but her father wasn't giving her time. "I buried him," she said, the aches in her body suggesting the lie.

"You buried him where?"

"Out by the barn. You can see where I dug if you want to go look."

"Thank God!" he said. "I thought we still had the whole rotten business to go through."

"What whole business?"

"Getting you to understand that the dog had to be destroyed. He was a menace."

"He was a hero. He tried to save me. He didn't know Hal was my brother."

"Did Hal kill him?"

"No, Hal's friend, Rick."

"What were they doing in the barn?"

"Looking for me, I guess."

He put the back of his hand against her cheek in a gesture of affection. "You're looking pretty peaked. Want to go back to sleep or get up and get something to eat?"

"I'll get up."

"Look," he said. "I know you're feeling bad, Bets, but it's just as well the dog's dead, and you'll get to feeling better soon."

"Will I, Pops?"

"I think so."

"Do you?"

"I'm feeling better now, yes." He kissed her forehead and left. She got herself out of bed, moving her limbs with great effort. It seemed she had gained a great deal of weight. Not just her weariness, but all the lies were beginning to weigh her down.

Her mother was sitting at the kitchen table waiting for the toast to pop up when Betsy got to the kitchen.

"Good morning, Mother," Betsy said.

"We were at the hospital most of the night," Mother said, accusing her. Dark crescents lay under her eyes.

"I wish it didn't happen—what happened with Hal," Betsy said, shaken by having both her parents angry with her. "I'm sorry he got hurt."

"How long did you keep that dog in the barn, Betsy?"

"Just—not very long."

"Does the shelter know you took him?"

"No. Don't tell them, please, Mother. I have a friend there who helped me. He'll get in trouble if you tell, and it wasn't his fault."

"Bill?"

"How do you know?"

"He called this morning, asking to speak to you. I told him to call back later. If he's old enough to work at the shelter, he ought to have had more sense than to let you take out a vicious dog."

"Zoro was only trying to protect me. He thought Hal was going to attack me."

"Betsy, don't you see what you did? You knew the dog didn't like people. You endangered other human beings recklessly."

"I thought I could train him. I could've. You didn't know Zoro. He was smart and he was—"

"You took chances with other people's lives, and you deliberately disobeyed me. I told you not to go near the shelter, and you've been over there a lot, haven't you?"

"Yes."

"Why didn't you listen to me?"

"I couldn't. I'm sorry, Mother. I really am."

Mother looked at her sadly. "I hope in the future you'll consider how what you want to do might affect others. That's all. I'm not going to give you more grief than you've already got over it."

But her mother's disappointment in her got through to Betsy and made her squirm in misery. How had she gotten herself into such a fix? It didn't even help knowing that it wasn't her parents' way to spread their anger out endlessly. They dumped it once and that was the end of it. Only, she had it inside her now. Part of her mind protested that it wasn't all her fault. Hal ought to bear some of the blame for what he had been doing in the barn. But she couldn't tell them about that. It didn't matter, anyway. She *had* done all the things of which her mother accused her, even more. She was guilty. But she remembered Zoro walking in the field with her last night, and she couldn't help being glad for those hours of pure happiness. They were probably the only ones he'd ever had in his entire life.

"Can I go to the shelter one last time and let Bill know what happened?" Betsy asked.

"All right. I want you home in half an hour, though. Then if you want to go to the hospital with us later, you can."

As she walked to the shelter, she thought about enlisting Bill's aid in caring for Zoro, but when she found him alone in the big garage where the emergency pens for injured animals or mothers with puppies were, she heard herself telling him, "Zoro's dead."

"Dead?" He looked shocked. "What happened?"

"My brother came into the barn with a friend." She didn't explain why they had come into the barn. "Zoro jumped my brother, and the other guy hit Zoro over the head and killed him. Now my brother's in the hospital and everybody's blaming me."

"Your brother's in the hospital? That's rotten. I knew I shouldn't of let you talk me into sneaking that dog out. It's my fault. I'm older than you. I'm the one who should've had better sense."

"It just happened, Bill. It was an accident."

"No. I knew it couldn't work out, and I let you go ahead. I don't know what got into me. I guess you're right, Betsy. I must really like you to let you talk me into something like that." He leaned one hand on the wall and bent his head, considering. Finally he said. "I'm going to tell Mr. Berrier what I did."

"What for?"

"To clear my conscience."

"But you might lose your job!"

"Yeah, I might. I'll deal with that when I have to."

She touched his arm. "You're not mad at me?"

"No," he said. "Why should I be mad at you? You're just a kid, and you got a thing in your head about that dog. I'm sorry about your brother, though, really sorry."

Instead of going straight home from the shelter, Betsy picked up Zoro's food and dishes from the barn and then set off for the appliance store. She was going to be late getting home, but with all the trouble she was in already, that hardly seemed to matter. She had left the side door open last night, and now she let herself into the back room of the store.

Zoro acted delighted to see her. He kept whimpering and licking his shoulder, which was badly swollen, and he seemed restless and hot, but he put his narrow head on her leg as if he took comfort from her presence. Only she didn't dare stay long. The half hour her mother had given her had to be up already. She left his food and water near him and left the side door unlocked again.

When she got home, she found her mother working on papers at the kitchen table, briefcase on the floor beside her. Mother didn't even comment on how long Betsy had been gone. She had probably been too busy to notice.

On the way to the hospital with her parents, Betsy sat in the back of the car. Thoughts scattered through her head. Suppose some stranger walked into the store—some kid climbed in the broken window, or somebody, hearing Zoro and thinking to save a trapped animal, went in there? Zoro would attack. Even with his wound, he was still dangerous.

"You can stop looking so guilty, Betsy," her mother said, turning around, talking as if she thought she understood what was going through Betsy's mind. "As long as you realize how irresponsible you were, you're on your way to behaving differently from now on, and nobody can expect more of you than that. Cheer up, huh?" Her mother reached over the back seat and took her hand. "Your hands are so cold, darling. Are you feeling sick?"

She almost blurted it out then, that Zoro was still alive, that she had lied and lied and lied. That someone else could still get hurt, killed maybe. What should she do? Call Mr. Berrier and tell him where to find Zoro. Call him from the hospital before anything happened. But then she'd be betraying Zoro. She was his chosen person, the only human he trusted. How could she, too, betray him? It was easier not to think at all, to blank everything out so that she didn't have to decide.

Sunday night the telephone rang, and her mother came smiling to where Betsy was sitting on the Danish lounger in front of the television set. "It's Bill. I think you have a boyfriend, Betsy."

"No," Betsy said flatly. She picked up the receiver in the kitchen and gave Bill a glum greeting.

"Listen, Betsy, I want you to tell me something."

"What?"

"The honest truth now. . . . Is Zoro dead?"

"No."

"I thought so. I started thinking you were probably lying because you acted so calm about it. . . . Where is he?"

"Please, Bill, I can't talk now."

"Then listen. . . . I'm going back to school next fall—not because of Mr. Berrier. I told him about helping you get Zoro out of the shelter and he wasn't too mad. Of course, he thinks Zoro's dead. Alive, that's a different story. But anyway—I started thinking about myself and what I really want to do with my life and I called my uncle. He says my father already talked to him. My father gave his permission for me to live at my uncle's and he'll pay my room and board—he doesn't know I'm already living there—just so I'll finish high school. I think things are going to work out for me now."

"That's good. That's great."

"Yeah, now what about you?"

"What about me?"

"You're a terrible liar, Betsy. You're a nice kid, but you're a terrible liar."

"I'm going to stop."

"You are? When? After Zoro kills some innocent person?"

"Bill, don't, please—"

"Betsy, tell me where he is. You have to. Don't you see that?"

Irresponsible—that was what her mother had said she was. Irresponsible to protect a dangerous dog. She shut her eyes. "He's in the appliance store down Blue Barns Road."

"That's the girl. I knew you were basically O.K. I'll talk to you tomorrow."

"Bill, what are you going to do?"

But he had hung up, and she knew very well what he was going to do. He'd tell Mr. Berrier and they'd go to the store with the catchpole. In a few hours it would be over. Zoro would be dead.

On Monday she couldn't get up to go to school. In her mind was the barn and Zoro watching her with honey-colored eyes full of devotion, the love and trust he had never felt for any other human. She had turned him in. She was a rotten person. She was weak or she would have been loyal to him, knowing she was all he had. All morning she watched her father through her window. He was planting bushes in the backyard.

At noontime her mother came into her bedroom in heels and her beige cotton suit.

"How come you're home early?" Betsy asked.

"I'm here on my lunch break. Bill called me." She sat down on the edge of Betsy's bed and looked at her sympathetically. "This story gets worser and worser," she said, trying to be cute.

Betsy turned her head away. "Did they kill him yet?"

"I know you loved Zoro, Betsy. I can understand how unhappy you must be now. But I want to tell you that what you did—finally—was the right thing. You were a responsible person—finally—who cares about other human beings. You did a hard thing, a terribly hard thing, and I am very proud of you, both your father and I are very proud of you."

"You are?"

"About Zoro and about Hal, too. He told me what he was doing in the barn. You didn't give him away. That was loyal. . . . Did Rick take the marijuana away?"

"No, I buried it."

"You buried it?" Her mother sounded amused.

"Yes, in the manure pile. That's where I told Dad I'd buried Zoro. I've been lying and lying. I'm so sick of lying. I'm never going to again."

"I hope not. It would be fine if you stuck to that resolution."

"Do you think Hal will hate me?"

"No, I think he'll be relieved. It cost him a lot of money which, in his present mood, I suspect he'll consider just punishment. As for Rick—I don't know."

"Maybe he'll try to beat me up."

"I doubt it. He'd know Hal wouldn't stand for that. Besides, Rick had no money invested in that deal. All he did was buy the pot for Hal. So he only lost whatever Hal was going to pay him for that transaction."

"O.K.," Betsy said. "Now tell me about Zoro."

Her mother shrugged. "They put him to sleep. Bill wanted to know if you wanted them to dispose of the body, or did you want to bury the dog some place."

Betsy lay rigid. She had known what she was going to hear, but now that she had heard it, it hurt so much she couldn't speak.

Her mother said, "When you were little, you used to have funerals for dead birds and squirrels. You had a whole animal cemetery in the backyard. I know you're not a baby any more, but I thought if you wanted him close by—your father says he'll dig the grave. . . . Anyway, it was sweet of Bill to think of asking, wasn't it?"

"There," her mother said. "There, there," as Betsy began to sob.

At the back of the bare yard was a mound of newly turned earth over the spot where her father had buried Zoro's dead body. Betsy carried the spade and the rosebush her mother had brought home for her out there after school the next afternoon.

As she stood holding the twiggy tripod of the rose called Peace and wondering if she dared dig into the soil where Zoro was buried, her father came up behind her.

"Let me," he said and dug a neat hole for her quickly.

"Would you say something, Popsy?"

"A funeral service for a dog?"

"Please."

He sighed. "All right. You ready, Betsy?" He spoke rapidly, as if he felt foolish. "Here lies a dog whose troubled spirit brought him to a bad end. Betsy loved him and did her best for him as far as she could go, and now she mourns for him. May his spirit find peace now and forever. Amen."

"He was a good dog," Betsy said. "Just people were mean to him, that's all. He should have been raised to love people. Then his life would have turned out all right."

"Mr. Berrier called, Bets. He says he's agreeable to your coming over to groom and walk the dogs when you've got free time, if you'd like to. I think he feels a little sorry for you."

"I'm not supposed to go near the shelter any more. Mother said."

"Well, if you think it wouldn't be too hard for you. I mean, if you think you can do it without getting emotionally involved with the animals.

We don't want you going through the same thing you went through with Zoro again."

"I couldn't. And even if I did get involved, so what? I don't want to just close my eyes and pretend everything's O.K. when it isn't. At least if I could help some animals be a little happier—that's something."

"I'd say so."

"It's hard to be a responsible adult, isn't it, Pops?"

"Very hard," he said and hugged her.

She went to get a pail of water to pour over the roots of the rosebush. She wanted to make sure it would flourish and grow beautiful enough to be worthy of the animal whose grave it marked. Someday, she promised herself, when she was grown and had her own home, she'd find a Doberman puppy, black with brown underneath and ears that stuck straight up. She would raise him to love people and she would name him Zoro.

About the Author

C. S. Adler was born in New York City and attended Hunter College High School and Hunter College. She has a master's degree in education from Russell Sage College and, for more than seven years, taught English in a middle school in Niskayuna, New York, where she and her husband raised three sons and now live. She is the author of three previous novels for young people, as well as of a number of published short stories for teenagers. She won the 1979 Golden Kite Award of the Society of Children's Book Writers.